Soul of a Monster 2

Lock Down Publications and
Ca$h Presents
Soul of a Monster 2
A Novel by Aryanna

Lock Down Publications

P.O. Box 870494
Mesquite, Tx 75187

Visit our website
www.lockdownpublications.com

Copyright 2019 by Aryanna
Soul of a Monster 2

First Edition September 2019
Printed in the United States of America

Lock Down Publications
Like our page on Facebook: Lock Down Publications @
www.facebook.com/lockdownpublications.ldp
Cover design and layout by: **Dynasty Cover Me**
Book interior design by: **Shawn Walker**
Edited by**: Kiera Northington**

Stay Connected with Us!

Text **LOCKDOWN** to 22828 to stay up-to-date
with new releases, sneak peeks, contests and more…

Submission Guideline.

Submit the first three chapters of your completed manuscript to ldpsubmissions@gmail.com, subject line: Your book's title. The manuscript must be in a .doc file and sent as an attachment. The document should be in Times New Roman, double-spaced and in size 12 font. Also, provide your synopsis and full contact information. If sending multiple submissions, they must each be in a separate email.

Have a story but no way to send it electronically? You can still submit to LDP/Ca$h Presents. Send in the first three chapters, written or typed, of your completed manuscript to:

LDP: Submissions Dept
Po Box 870494
Mesquite, Tx 75187

DO NOT send original manuscript. Must be a duplicate.

Provide your synopsis and a cover letter containing your full contact information.

Thanks for considering LDP and Ca$h Presents.

Dedication:

This book is dedicated to my everything because you inspire me.

Acknowledgements:

I give all glory to God for making me a storyteller. It's a gift that I don't take for granted. I wanna thank my soulmate and better half for rocking with me nonstop. I love you more! I wanna thank my family for their love and support because it never waivers. I wanna thank my extended family (my in-laws) for loving what I love and giving life to her. I wanna thank my fans for the constant love and continued support. Each and every one of you means the world to me. I wanna thank my LDP family for rocking with me. Shout out to my haters!!! I gotta shout out the real niggas that make a difference. Polo, Pree, Squeeze, A.J, Uncle Lin - founders of the HYPE program (Helping Youth Prevail Everywhere). It takes strong men to change their lives and then work towards helping other people change theirs. Each one teach one! Never let prison limit you in any way. Take your program beyond the walls of Buckingham Correctional Center and empower the youth. I love what you all do, and I'm proud of you. I gotta shout out all the people who contribute to making me what I am. Thank you! Shout out to Nikka "stank stank" Smith. The real Baby D (#1193541). I gotta show love to my baby girl (mini me) Aryanna, and her best friend Ka'nyia Green. R.I.P to SHA'KEZ AMIR GREEN (Gone but never forgotten). I know you all are struggling with your loss, but he's in a better place. R.I.P to MALAKYH PER-

SON. Last, but never least, I gotta thank my sister, Big Byrd. I love you like no other! You're my world on a different level, and there's not enough words to sum up our relationship. It's you and me 'til the end!!

Aryanna

Chapter 1
October 2020
Dollar

Neither my dreams nor nightmares had any scenes in them where my ex-wife and my current wife appeared side-by-side. It wasn't a sick fantasy, not even one where revenge was the motivation, because as much as I hated my ex, I'd soon as just forget her than anything else. The look on Honey's face said forgetting for either of us wouldn't be possible, at least not on this subject.

"Dameian, did-did you just say that you used to be married to her? To my-my sister?" Honey asked in disbelief.

"Wow, he actually told you his real name? It took me years to learn that secret," Amanda said bitterly.

I cut my eyes in her direction, wanting nothing more than to lift her soul out of her chest with my bare hands, but knowing that wasn't possible right now.

"Like I stated a moment ago when I admitted to shooting her, I had no idea that Amanda/Katie, or whatever the fuck her name is, was your sister," I replied.

"Is her sister, as in present tense. I know you see me standing right here in front of you, no matter how much you wish it wasn't true, Dameian."

"Bitch—""

"Don't!" Honey said, stepping in between her sister and me to prevent my attack.

Had it not been for the pain on Honey's face, the only thing that would've stopped me from choking the smirk off her sister's face would've been a bullet. Despite it being years since I'd laid eyes on Katie, I wanted to hurt her just as badly as I had the day I'd shot her, but she wasn't worth me causing my wife any more pain.

"Wow, I'm impressed, sis. Never before have I seen someone with the ability to control the infamous Dameian Morgan," Amanda said, chuckling.

"Amanda, shut up and get in the damn car before I forget you're my sister."

"I'm not getting in the car with that psycho! Did you miss the part where I said he shot me in the neck, and left me for dead?" Amanda asked.

"No. I heard that part, but I didn't hear the reason why though, because I'm sure that only makes the story more interesting."

"Ask her," I said, turning around and walking away.

"Dollar, stop…Dollar, get in the car!" Honey yelled after me.

It bothered me to ignore her, but I needed to put some space in between me and Katie. Of course, Katie wasn't her real name, so I had to stop thinking of her like that. Names didn't matter though, and I knew that better than anybody. Her name didn't change her past any more than it did mine, but if I didn't get ahold of myself, I was gonna let the past fuck up my future. I didn't want that, any more than I wanted to be walking away from my wife, which meant I had to figure out what to do next. To say this situation caught me flat-footed was the biggest understatement of my life! I pulled my phone out with the intention of calling an Uber to come get me, but instead, I found myself calling the one person I knew could help with this chaos.

"It's me," I said, when she answered.

"What's wrong, you bored with the road trip already?" Aubrey asked, laughing.

"Sis."

"You sound way too serious this early in the morning, Dollar, what's wrong?" she asked.

"Katie."

Just speaking that name took both of us back almost seven years. I could still remember when I'd introduced Katie and Aubrey, and the surprise I felt at the fact that they'd actually hit it off. I'd never been the sucker-for-love type, but there had been something about the five foot three, hundred and fifty-three pound, brown-eyed beauty I'd met by chance at the bar of a popular night spot in New York. I was there on business, and blending in was a part of that, so I'd offered to buy her a drink. At least that's what I'd told myself then. But, I admitted the truth when we were fucking up her headboard a couple hours later. Somehow, that one-night stand turned into a four-year relationship that ended in tragedy. At least, that's what I'd thought until a little while ago.

"Have you been drinking? The last time I heard you say that name, you were sloppy drunk and I had to smack the shit out of you," Aubrey said.

"No, I haven't been drinking, but I damn sure wish I was drunk."

"Okay, so what made you say her name?" she asked, confused.

"Because, I just saw her."

"Dollar, that's not—"

"Do you really think I would've called you on some impossible shit, or some wild hallucinations?" I asked impatiently.

For a moment, only silence was spoken between us on the phone.

"Oh, wow. Okay, tell me more."

"I'm not sure you're ready for more," I replied honestly.

"Yeah, well, you know I'm not about to let your ass off the phone after you dropped that bomb."

The sudden roar of a car's engine behind me got my attention, and a few moments later, Honey swerved to a stop in front of me.

"She's Honey's sister. I gotta go," I said, hanging up as my wife stepped out of the car.

"Dameian, you know I love you, right?" she asked, ejecting the clip from the pistol in her hands.

"Yes, I know that."

"And, you know I would do anything for you, right?" she asked, swiftly ejecting the bullet from the chamber.

"I think I know where this is going."

"Yep, I'ma put a part in your muthafuckin' head if you don't get in the damn car, so we can get far away from here," she stated.

Despite the obvious size advantage of my six foot three, two hundred forty pounds to her five foot four, hundred and fifty pounds, I knew she had enough crazy in her to try and pistol whip me right here on prison grounds. It wouldn't be a smart move for her, but it was still sexy knowing she'd do it.

"Just shoot him and let's go," Amanda said from the passenger seat.

Honey quickly shook her head at me to discourage any retort I had, giving me a feeling that I was gonna have a tongue full of holes by nightfall. I didn't say shit though. I simply got in the backseat. To my surprise, she passed ne the gun and ammunition when she got back behind the wheel.

"Have you lost your goddamn mind? You just gave him a gun," Amanda said angrily.

"Relax, he's not gonna shoot you," Honey replied.

"Fuck that, I'm—"

Before she could step one foot out of the door she'd opened, Honey had slid the car into first gear, and gunned the engine. If Amanda wanted out now, she was guaranteed to fuck up her pretty face.

"Pull over and let me out, Tabitha, I'm not playing," she demanded.

"What's with you using people's government names? Let's get some shit straight, sis, you can call me Tab like you've been doing or Honey, but don't let my full name come out of your mouth. And, don't call my husband by any other name than Dollar."

"Are you two even legally married?" Amanda asked.

I could tell by the way Honey's hand tensed up on the steering wheel that her patience was running low, but it wasn't my place to interfere in a family dispute.

"Do you feel like I'm less likely to shoot you if you piss me off?" Honey asked.

"Shoot me for what? I was just asking a question, because your husband doesn't care much for doing things legally."

"So, were you two married legally?" Honey retorted.

"Unfortunately," Amanda replied.

"Well, that's proof that he does what he wants to do, and don't be arrogant enough to think you're the last woman who could get him to the altar," Honey said.

I didn't even try to muffle my laughter, which of course made Amanda give me a dirty look over her shoulder.

"So, was this your plan, Dollar, marry my sister to find out where I was?" Amanda asked aggressively.

"Not hardly. I married Honey because I love her, and as I stated earlier, I had no fucking idea she was your sister."

"Love her?" Amanda scoffed sarcastically.

"You got one more time to get on some uppity shit in this car, bitch, and I'ma beat you," Honey warned angrily.

"I'm not being uppity, Tab, I just doubt Dollar is capable of loving anyone or anything, except his job. He did tell you what he really does for a living, right?"

"No, he didn't tell me, I saw it first-hand. That's how we met," Honey replied.

"Still picking up chicks at work, huh, Dollar?" Amanda asked, shaking her head.

The look Honey gave me in the rearview mirror had a lot of questions, but now it was my turn to shake my head in indication to leave it alone. To think that she wouldn't get the full story out of me was simply delusional, but this car wasn't big enough for all that shit.

"You know, Amanda, you've got a lot of questions, but you need to be answering some your damn self. For starters, how the fuck do I not know that you were married and your husband shot you?" Honey asked.

"I don't know, he wasn't worth talking about."

I could tell by the side eye Honey slid in her sister's direction that she didn't believe that vague answer any more than I did. Personally, I didn't care, but I knew bullshit when I heard it.

"Why did he shoot you?" Honey asked.

In response to this question, Amanda turned around in her seat and looked me directly in the eyes. For a moment, the anger and bitterness were gone, replaced by a guilt that was too believable for even my cynical mind to call bullshit. She didn't have to speak for me to know what she was thinking. Not because we were still in tune with one another, but because I know she was replaying the day that changed everything.

"I-I cheated on him, and he caught me," she replied softly.

I could feel Honey's eyes on me, but my gaze stayed locked with Amanda's.

"Why do I get the feeling that there's more?" Honey asked slowly.

"Because there is," I replied.

"The person I cheated with was someone Dollar knew and trusted, which is rare because he doesn't trust anyone, and—"

"He was something like a father to me," I corrected, trying to control my anger.

"If he valued your relationship the same way then he wouldn't have stuck his dick in me, but you never considered that."

"Sure I did, and that's why I cut his dick and balls off before I killed him," I said, smiling at the memory.

"So, you did kill him?" Amanda asked.

"What the hell would make you doubt that he would? I mean, you do know him, right?" Honey asked.

"Yeah, I know him, but somehow I thought Dollar would forgive him."

"I don't forgive," I said sincerely.

That statement had everyone in the car quiet, no doubt contemplating the question of what my next move would be. Amanda gave her thoughts away when she looked down at the gun in my hand.

"When did all this shit happen?" Honey asked.

"Three years ago," Amanda replied, looking me in the eyes.

"If I remember correctly, that's when you disappeared for a year, only to resurface out here charged with murder," Honey said.

Hearing this made me raise my eyebrow in surprise.

"Murder, huh?" I asked.

"A mistake, as evidenced by the fact that I was just released. Only one of us had blood on their hands."

"I wouldn't go that far, Amanda, because you told me you got off on a technicality," Honey said.

"Whose side are you on, sis?" Amanda asked, irritated.

"I'll answer that in a minute," she replied, pulling into the Best Western parking lot.

"What are you doing?" I asked.

"You don't really think we're about to take all this drama back to Mississippi, do you? Nah, we 'bout to hash some shit out right now," Honey declared, getting out of the car.

I could tell Amanda wanted to object to being left alone with me, but her savior had already disappeared inside the motel. I slammed the clip back into the gun and pulled the slide just to be an asshole. Seeing Amanda flinch was worth it though.

"I won't be mad if you run, I'm good at hitting moving targets," I said, smiling.

She apparently didn't find my offer appealing or funny, because she simply turned around in her seat and stared out the window. A couple minutes later, Honey returned and drove us around back to the room she'd rented. I had no idea what she hoped to accomplish, but I followed her and Amanda inside. Once we were all behind the closed door, the awkwardness kicked up several notches for some reason, but no one spoke to ease the tension.

"Baby, what are you hoping to accomplish?" I asked.

"It's real simple, the truth needs to come out so that we can all move on," Honey replied.

"There's nothing to move on from, just keep your dog on a leash and we'll be good," Amanda stated.

"Bae, let me see that gun," Honey requested, holding her hand out.

I knew my wife well enough to know this was a bad idea, but I still passed her the Glock .17.

"You've been hanging around him too long if you're resorting to using guns to intimidate people, but either way, I'm not scared of you," Amanda said.

Honey didn't say a word as she pulled the silencer from her pocket and screwed it on. Amanda may have thought she was bullshitting, but I knew better. The look in her eyes spelled determination.

"Honey, listen—"

"Shhh, not your turn to speak, bae, I need to talk to my sister first. Amanda, I'm gonna ask you something, but first I need to stress the fact that you need to be one hundred percent honest, not ninety-nine percent, but one-hundred, understand?"

"Sure, Tab, what do you wanna know about me and your husband?"

"Who's Kyla's dad?" Honey asked.

I had no idea who they were talking about, but the terror on Amanda's face spoke to the importance of whoever Kyla was.

"Tab, don't," Amanda replied weakly.

"I asked you a question, sis."

"I know you did and we can talk about it later," Amanda insisted.

Honey quickly took aim at her left leg.

"Answer the question, Amanda, who's Kyla's dad? Who's your baby's father?"

"Baby?" I asked quickly.

Amanda immediately closed her eyes and shook her head.

Aryanna

"Fuck you, Tab," she said softly.
The next sound was the gun going off.

Chapter 2
Honey

I wasn't sure what I'd feel before pulling the trigger and putting a bullet in my own sister, but now that I'd done it, I knew. I felt nothing. The one thing I couldn't stand was a liar, and it seemed like every other sentence out of Amanda's mouth was a goddamn lie. When she'd come out her face with the bullshit about why she'd never even mentioned Dollar, I knew she'd been lying, and I had a hunch why.

"Y-you fucking shot me, you bitch!" she cried from her position on the floor.

"I told you to keep it one hundred, but you thought I was bullshitting. Now you know better. I still want an answer though, so who—"

"I don't know!" she yelled, crying and clutching her calf as her blood stained the carpet.

"You don't know?" I repeated skeptically.

"Honey, do you know what you're doing?" Dollar asked, looking at me closely.

Did I know what I was doing? Honestly, I was moving off of pure instinct and adrenaline right now, but it felt good, so I was gonna roll with it.

"I got this, bae," I replied, winking at him. "Amanda, I'm gonna ask you again, and then I'm gonna give you a matching hole in your right leg."

"I don't, I don't know who her dad is," she replied, in between her deep breaths.

"Could it be Dollar?"

"Mine?" he asked, dumbfounded.

I doubted my husband would hesitate in shooting a pregnant bitch, and it might just turn out that he shot the bitch pregnant with his baby.

"Tabitha, please," Amanda sobbed, looking at me with her heart in her eyes.

I loved my sister, and I'd always done everything I could to protect or help her, despite the fact that her father had raped my mother. What I wouldn't and couldn't do was allow her to fuck up the happiness I'd found with Dollar. Not no way, not no how. I moved the still smoking pistol in my hand until it was fixed on her right leg, preparing to make good on my threat.

"Okay, okay, yes! Yes, Kyla might be Dollar's!" she said, holding her hand up as if it would stop a bullet.

"Might be?" I pressed, seeing the truth in her eyes.

"Pr-probably is," she finally conceded.

One glance at the shock on Dollar's face told me he fully comprehended the magnitude of what was just revealed. Somehow, the truth hanging in the air made the gun in my hand heavier, forcing me to let my arm drop to my side. I was trying to wrap my mind around the big picture, but it seemed too fucking amazing to be true. Not only had my sister been married to, fucked by, and shot by the love of my life, but nine out of ten my niece was now my stepdaughter! How the fuck was I supposed to deal with that? I had no idea where to begin, but it couldn't be right here, right now.

"Put-put pressure on it, I'll go get some stuff to bandage you up," I said, turning towards the door.

"Honey, wait—"

I don't know what words Dollar was prepared to use to make this situation better, but he'd have to save them for later. I hurried to the car, threw myself behind the wheel, and tossed the gun on the seat beside me before starting the engine. I damn near slid into a parked car as I fishtailed wildly, before the tires grabbed the pavement and shot the car towards the exit. I had no idea where I was going or what all I needed, but it took me a few minutes to realize that I was too blinded by my tears to see the road in front of me. I pulled over and tried taking deep breaths to calm myself down, but it was no use and I dissolved into tears. I spent no less than ten minutes, crying hysterically before I was able to pull it together and get my phone out of my pocket. It took three tries to dial the number that I wanted, but finally I heard it ringing in my ear.

"Hi, sweetheart, how's the road trip?"

"M-Mommy," I sobbed.

"Tabitha, what's wrong? Are you hurt? Is Dollar hurt? Talk to me, baby."

I knew I was scaring my mother, but it still took me a couple minutes to get myself together enough to make sense. In a wild rush of profanity and emotion, I managed to explain what was going on. Truthfully, my mom was the last person I should've called, because any mention of Amanda reminded her of what she'd experienced at the hands of our father. The sad fact was that even at thirty-eight years old, sometimes, a woman just needed her mother. My mom, being the saint that she was, listened and comforted me until I stopped feeling like I would come out of my skin at any moment.

"W-what am I gonna do, Mom?" I asked, once I laid the facts at her feet.

"Do? Well, baby, when it comes to the past, what exactly can you do? What's done is done, and all we can do is pray for the strength to move forward. As for the future, well, you don't let it be controlled by the past. You do everything you can to make your future what you want it to be, and you understand that the rest is up to God."

"But, Mom, what if—"

"Tabitha, you know that what-ifs are a waste of time, so why indulge in them? You can handle all that's happened, because God never puts more on you than you can handle, and he's given you someone to share your burdens. Dollar loves you, of that I'm sure, so go to your husband and let him love you," she instructed.

"I love you, Mom," I said, smiling through my tears because nothing in the world could make her pessimistic.

"I love you too, baby. Call me when you need me."

I hung up and took a few moments to gather myself. When I looked in the mirror, I thought I looked entirely too much like a wet cat, but I was still sexy. Once I got back on the road, I decided to take a page from Dollar's book and troll the local hospital for a nurse that I could convince to help me. No sooner had I arrived, I spotted a funny-built bitch in black scrubs, getting out of her car.

"Excuse me, miss, can you help me?" I asked.

"I can try. What do you need?"

"Actually, it's my sister who's in need, but she's at our motel right now," I replied.

"Ok, well, you'll have to bring her in if you want her to get treatment."

"Well, the thing is that she can't come to the hospital, because they have to report gunshot victims and—"

"And if she doesn't want it reported, then that means she's probably involved in things I want no part of," she said, turning away from me.

I couldn't explain why her dismissive attitude pissed me off so bad, but before I knew it, I had the gun in my hand and I was out of the car. I glanced around quickly before walking up on her and jamming the silencer in her back roughly.

"If you so much as whistle, bitch, I'll blow your spine through your stomach, understand?" I asked.

She nodded shakily.

"Turn around and waddle your big ass back to my car," I demanded, helping her turn around before pushing her towards my open door.

"Pl-please, I have k-kids."

"You getting dick? Built like that? I guess there really is somebody for everybody. If you weren't so dumb, you could've added something to your kid's college fund, but now you'll just be doing a good service. Now get in," I said, pushing her across the driver's seat.

Once she maneuvered her girth into a sitting position, I climbed in, tucked the gun under my left leg away from her reach, and pulled off.

"All I need you to do is bandage my sister up, and then you can go on your way. It's not anything major, just a bullet to the leg."

"It'll be serious if an artery was hit," she informed me.

"Ain't you just full of fun facts," I replied, pressing down on the gas a little harder.

The last thing I wanted was for Amanda to fuck around and bleed out. I still loved her lying ass. Part of me was shocked I'd actually shot her, but being around Dollar had released me from society's shackles that said shooting people was wrong. Sometimes putting a hot slug in a muthafucka got results that were otherwise unattainable. The sudden sound of sirens forced my eyes to drop to the speedometer, where to my horror I saw I was doing eighty miles an hour.

"What's the speed limit?" I asked, checking my rearview mirror to find that the sirens were definitely meant for me.

"Forty-five miles an hour."

"Fuck!" I exclaimed, mad at myself.

As badly as I wanted to stand on the gas pedal with both feet, I knew that wasn't my smartest move, so I pulled off down a side street and stopped.

"You said you got kids, right? Well, if you want them to live through the day, you'll play this shit cool," I said calmly.

While keeping my eyes on the rearview mirror, I slowly moved the pistol from beneath my leg, and slowly un-screwed the silencer. If shit got ugly, I really didn't want anyone to hear, but the silencer made the gun too long for a quick draw. What I wasn't about to do was lose my life on some side street in Nowhereville, Tennessee. After what seemed like an eternity a tall, broad-shouldered white guy emerged from the cop car, and headed in our direction.

"Do you know how fast you were driving?" he asked.

"Uh, no, but if I was speeding I apologize, Officer."

"You can save your apologies for the judge, but you can give me your license and, Kr-Kristen, is that you?" he asked, leaning further down so he could get a better look in the car.

My grip on the gun in my left hand tightened instantly as I turned to look at my passenger.

"H-hey, Dave," she replied.

Of course, I would have to get the one cop in Mayberry that knew this bitch.

"I thought you'd be at work by now, instead of joy riding with Dale Jr. here," he said.

"Yeah, I'm headed to work now."

"You are? But, you were coming from the direction of the hospital when I lit you up," he replied slowly.

When I looked back at him, I could see the confusion on his face and just below that was something worse. Doubt. That was all I needed to see before I raised the gun and fired twice, hitting him point-blank in the face. Before his body could get comfortable on the ground, I was out of the car and snatching off all the components to his body cam. I looked up just in time to see Nurse Fat Ass trying to scurry away, but two bullets in her back halted her progress. I wanted to make sure she was dead, but time was something I'd just run out of. I jumped back in the car and pulled off as fast as I could, cussing myself out the entire way back to the motel. I didn't bother to park. I barely even let the car come to a complete stop before I hit the ground running. I burst through the motel room door to find a sight that instantly made me raise my gun again.

"Why the fuck don't you have a shirt on?" I asked Dollar, levelling the gun at his chest.

"Because I used it to stop the bleeding, since your little ass was taking so long. I could've just let the bitch die, but I somehow thought that would put me in this same situation of being on the opposite end of a gun in your hand."

I let my arm drop and tucked the gun into the waist of my shorts.

"We gotta go, and I do mean now," I said.

"What happened?" he asked, eyes narrowing on my face.

"I don't have time to explain, but two people are dead, one was a cop, and I pulled the trigger."

"You're fucked then," Amanda said from her spot on the floor.

"Not while I'm around," Dollar stated confidently.

I loved how even at the height of chaos he never showed fear, never got shaky like most niggas who play at being a gangsta until shit hits the fan. He was different and that was what I needed.

"Do a quick wipe down of the shit you touched while I put Amanda in the car," he instructed, already moving.

I grabbed a towel and got to work, moving swiftly. By the time I was done, Amanda was stretched out across the backseat and Dollar was behind the wheel waiting. I got in, and we got gone.

Chapter 3
Dollar

"Tell me what happened," I demanded, trying to drive at a rate of speed that didn't indicate fleeing from the law.

"I went to the local hospital to find a nurse to help Amanda, and I was gonna pay her for her discretion, but the bitch ain't wanna act right. So, I put the gun on her and made her get in the car."

"Kidnapping people in broad daylight now? You really have been around him too long," Amanda said.

"Not now, bitch," Honey warned.

"Okay, so tell me how everything went bad," I said, staying on topic.

"I was speeding, we got pulled over and I shot the cop, because it was clear he wasn't about to believe the story we were kickin' to him. It turns out he knew the nurse I'd snatched up. When I shot him, I jumped out of the car to snatch his body cam and that's when the nurse tried to make a run for it, which forced me to shoot her."

"Wow, sis, you've changed," Amanda said.

"Bitch, didn't I say not now?" Honey growled, half turning in her seat.

I put my arm on hers to stop her from leaping into the backseat and giving her sister a much-needed ass whooping, but only because now wasn't the time for all of that.

"Katie, she already shot your silly ass once, so I'd advise you to chill," I said, looking at her in the rearview mirror.

"Oh, so you're back to calling her Katie now? Isn't that cute!"

"Bae, please stay focused. I need to know where the shooting took place, and I know you don't know your way around here, so just be as specific as you can," I said, pulling my phone out and calling Aubrey.

"About two-three miles east of the hospital, heading towards the motel," she replied.

As soon as Aubrey answered, I began relaying the details before she could get a word in about my ex-wife. I needed her focused on what was important. There would be time to get to the woman in the backseat later.

"Alright, I'll erase any and all traffic footage I can find with your wife in it, as well as the car you're riding in. Anything else?" Aubrey asked.

"Once you're done with that, I want you to report this car stolen. We should be out of Tennessee in about an hour, so wait until then."

"Where are you going?" she asked.

"Mississippi for now, but I'll call you once I get there."

"Be safe," she said.

"Trust me, the only threat to my safety is currently bleeding in the backseat."

"Tell me you're not riding around with that bitch's body right now, because—"

"No, I'm not, and I'll fill you in later," I replied, hanging up.

"Why didn't you tell Aubrey I said hi?" Katie asked.

"Wait, you know Aubrey too?" Honey asked, looking at me despite the question being directed to the backseat.

"Of course I do, but I haven't seen her in a while for obvious reasons," Katie replied.

"Seen her," Honey said slowly, staring a hole in the side of my head.

There was a lot of shit I needed to tell Honey, but I'd preferred to do it without her sister's presence or interference. It was becoming evident that I should've told Katie this when we had our conversation over the bandaging of her bullet wound, but there had been another more important topic to discuss. I was still trying to come to terms with all of that.

"Honey, my past with Katie is complicated. I was a different person in a lot of ways, but her betrayal forced me to shut a lot of doors when it came to letting people into my personal life. You've broken down some of the barriers I put up, and I promise you're the only woman who has. I need you not to judge our relationship now, based off of my relationship with her in the past."

I'd taken her hand in mine while making this plea and the strength of her grip on my fingers gave me hope that she was hearing me. My love for Honey was beyond measurement, and there was nothing in my past to compare it to. As long as I could make my wife understand that then I knew whatever we had to face we could face it together.

"I understand what you're saying, bae, it's just-it's just so fucking weird for all of this to happen and be a complete coincidence," Honey replied.

"I swear to you, I had no idea about your connection to Katie or the fact that she was still alive. Everything that happened between us is real, and built on the right foundation."

"Aww, that's so sweet," Katie said, from the backseat.

"You really do want me to shoot you again, huh?" Honey asked, smiling like she'd enjoy nothing more.

"I want you to open your eyes to your husband's bullshit! Okay, let's say he didn't know who you were in relation to me, that still doesn't change the fact that he's a killer. He's not a good person, Tab."

The way Honey looked at me and smiled made me smile at her in return, like there was a secret that only the two of us knew.

"I know exactly who my husband is, trust me. I love him for exactly who he is."

"And I love you too, bae," I said sincerely.

"Well, I love the fact that my daughter hasn't been tainted by him or his lifestyle. You might not agree with my decision to keep Kyla a secret from this monster, but I know she's better off never knowing that Dameian Morgan existed," Katie said.

The truth in her words didn't allow for anger to take ahold of me, although I could see Honey's rage clear as day on her beautiful face. I continued to hold her hand, hoping she would simply let her sister's comments go, but I could feel the heat coming from her pores. She was pissed!

"You call my husband a monster? You say that Kyla was better off not knowing her daddy? So, why then have you always tried to facilitate a relationship between me and the monster who raped my mother? Why can't I be better off not knowing that piece of shit, instead of you trying to convince me of how much he's changed? Answer that, you hypocritical bitch!"

In the rearview, I could see Katie open her mouth to speak, but no words came out.

"Speechless? Not you," I taunted.

"I'm not surprised. Now you know why I've never called her Katie, because that's what her precious father calls her," Honey said.

I nodded my head in understanding, while still waiting on some type of justification or tirade to come from the backseat. It didn't come though, and we rode on in a silence that was loud without individual thoughts. I existed and thrived in chaotic situations, but the last couple hours have been on some unbelievable shit. As I'd been trying to stop Katie's leg from bleeding, it has still been hard to wrap my mind around the fact that I'd been actually touching her. My mind kept screaming that I was touching a dead woman, but eventually, I had to admit it was simply wishful thinking. To my own horror and amazement, I was starting to question if I even wished her dead anymore. The basis for this thought stemmed from the knowledge that had I known she was pregnant, I wouldn't have shot her in that motel room and left her for dead. The possibility of her being pregnant with my child would've saved her life until a DNA test was done, and then who knows what would've happened. All I know now was she'd given birth to a child that was more than likely mine, and given the fact that she was all my daughter had had, I was second guessing wishing death on her. No doubt she deserved it, but little Kyla deserved only good vibes and love.

"I can't feel my leg," Katie complained.

"We'll be in Mississippi in a couple hours, and you'll get seen by a doctor," Honey replied.

"Why Mississippi?"

"You ask too many questions," Honey said, pulling out her phone.

I assumed she was texting Denise and Savannah, so they'd be prepared for our newest patient in the psych ward.

"Are you sure it's a good idea to take her to the house where everybody else is?" I asked.

"No, but I'm taking care of it."

"Just dump me in the alley," Katie said sarcastically.

"Tempting, but I won't give you the satisfaction of playing the victim. I'll nurse you back to health, and then we'll decide where to go from there," Honey stated.

I wanted to give my input on the upside of an alley dump, but I kept my mouth shut and my eyes on the road. A little more than two hours later, I eased the car to a stop in the driveway next to my black Ferrari.

"Wow, whose house is this?" Katie asked, clearly impressed.

"Your baby daddy," Honey replied, getting out of the car, and going into the house.

I could tell Katie felt as uncomfortable as I did, but the plus was that at least she wasn't screaming about me trying to kill her.

"Is this really your house?"

"I don't understand why that surprises you, but yeah, it's mine," I replied.

"It's just that you've always lived by the seat of your pants, at least when I knew you. This house makes you seem…domesticated. That's not a word I would've ever used to describe you."

"People change," I said simply, looking at her in the rearview mirror.

"Do you really expect me to believe you've changed?" she asked skeptically.

"I honestly don't care what you believe. I've never had a problem with the man that I am."

"Yeah, but that was probably before you knew about Kyla. I know how bad you wanted to be a dad, Dollar."

Her statement brought back the memories of conversations we'd had about having kids, weighing the pros and cons of creating a family, given my lifestyle. We'd both wanted kids, but we were both realistic about all the things that could go wrong if we brought a child into the world. So, we'd left it up to fate after a few years, forgoing all forms of birth control and accepting that whatever was meant to be would be. It was clear that either God or the devil had a sense of humor.

"Is she my daughter?" I asked, locking eyes with her.

"How many times are you gonna ask me that? I thought we already covered this during our little come to Jesus in the motel room."

"It's been years since I've seen or talked to you, but I still know when you're full of shit, Katie. No more games. Is Kyla mine?"

I could see the lie in her eyes before she opened her mouth, but I saw her rethink whatever she was about to say. Her earlier tirade about her daughter being better off without me had told me more than she wanted, because up until that point, she'd claimed to be unsure if I'd fathered her child. While I'd been working to stop her leg from bleeding, she'd said there was a good chance, but she wouldn't one hundred percent commit one way or another. Given her infidelity, it should've been easy enough to believe what she'd said, but it just didn't ring true. Her not knowing who the father of her child was wasn't something she could've lived with.

"I don't see what difference it makes. Are you really gonna argue against the truth that she's better off without you?" she asked.

"I won't know the answer to that until I know everything about her, how she's being raised, and what her life has been like. Before we get to that, we need to start at the beginning."

She hesitated for a few more moments, but at this point we knew it was pointless.

"Yes, she's your daughter, Dollar. She looks just like you, except she's got a high yellow complexion."

I didn't really know what to say right now. It was one thing to treat Iree like my child, but it was completely different to have an actual child of my own. Undoubtedly, my life would change, but I couldn't imagine how drastically. Seeing Honey come back out of the house with Denise and Savannah in tow brought my mind back to the present problems that needed addressing. I got out the car and helped Katie from the backseat before scooping her up into my arms.

"Dollar, where the hell is your shirt?" Iree hollered from the porch.

I ignored her and focused on the women in front of me.

"I thought you normally left people where you shot them," Denise said.

"I didn't shoot her."

My statement made all eyes swing towards Honey, who simply ignored the questioning stares.

"It don't matter who shot her. This is my sister, Amanda, and I need you two to take care of her. Amanda, this is Denise and Savannah, a licensed nurse and doctor that are privately employed by us."

"My name is Katie, and I'll kindly ask you two to disregard whatever she wants, just don't let me die."

"Dollar, take her upstairs," Honey instructed.

"Thanks, sis," Katie replied sarcastically, blowing her a kiss.

I headed for the house before Honey could say or do something ignorant.

"Will you stop antagonizing her?" I asked.

"Why, I've done it our whole lives."

"You're smart enough to know that shit is different now, so just chill," I advised, holding her tighter so I didn't drop her going up the stairs.

"And this is?" Iree asked, crossing her arms over her chest, and turning on her resting bitch face.

"I'm Katie, Tabitha's sister, and you are?"

"I'm Iree, Dollar's daughter."

Katie's head snapped around so fast that she almost head-butted me in the chin. The look she was giving me said she was seconds away from taking a swing at me anyway.

"How the fuck do you have a grown daughter that I don't know about?" she asked heatedly.

"Why would you know about me? And the way you asked that suggests that you have an issue with my existence, which will get your ass whooped," Iree stated, taking an aggressive step forward.

"Yo, chill! Both of you!" I demanded.

"Bruh, you better get that bitch, because I don't care if she is Honey's sister! She ain't got one more chance to be disrespectful, and that hole in her leg ain't gonna stop me from thumping her ass either!"

"Dollar, take her upstairs. Iree come with me," Honey said, taking her by the hand and leading her into the house.

I could feel the tension in Katie's body, but she wisely kept her mouth shut as I made my way inside, and up the stairs with her. I carried her to the last bedroom on this floor which gave her privacy and exclusive access to the porch up here. As soon as I laid her on the bed, Denise and Savannah got to work on the wound to her leg. I could tell by the stare Katie was levelling at me that we were due for a long talk, but I put that on pause as I went in search of a shirt. Once I had that on, I called Aubrey to get the latest and let her know we'd made it safety. My next order of business was to find out what my wife's plan was, and I found her with Iree beneath a cloud of weed smoke in my office.

"You need this," Iree said, passing me a blunt and shaking her head sadly.

"I appreciate the sympathy, but can you tell me why you were on your bullshit from the jump?"

"She's upset that Rain is leaving, and she figured correctly that it had everything to do with our visitor," Honey said.

"Rain's leaving? Does that mean the whole family is leaving?" I asked confused, hitting the blunt.

"Yeah, we're leaving shortly."

"We?" I asked quickly.

"And, that's my cue," Iree said, getting out of the chair and leaving the room.

I continued to smoke the blunt in my hand while waiting impatiently for my wife to make sense of the shit she'd said.

"I'm going with them back to Alabama, just to get them settled in and make sure my mom is okay. Just the mention of my sister forces her to think about the past, and it's not fair for me to do that to her. I promise, I won't be gone long."

"I understand, baby, I really do. You don't expect me to stay here with Katie though do you?" I asked.

"I mean that's up to you. Regardless of how much I hate the situation, you two still share a child and some very complicated history. I would appreciate if you could somehow manage to work through that, so I don't have to shoot her again."

We both knew she wasn't asking me for something small, but it wasn't the first time she'd asked me to do something that went completely against what I believed in.

"You know I got you, sweetheart, just don't be gone long."

"I love you too much to be gone long, you know that. Plus, I don't think knowing the truth makes Iree any less hostile towards my sister," she replied.

"I'll watch them both, I promise."

Chapter 4
Honey

"Do you have to amputate?" I asked, walking into the room where Denise and Savannah were attending to my sister.

"Amputate?" Amanda repeated hollowly.

"If you think that'll be easier, I can get a bone saw without a problem," Savannah replied, looking at me.

"Whoa, hold up, ain't nobody cutting my damn leg off! You two just said the bullet went straight through, and I should heal fine."

"Calm your dramatic ass down before I shoot you again," I said, pulling out the Taurus .357 Dollar had just given me.

"So, you really did shoot her?" Denise asked, wide eyed.

"Yep, and I'll do it again if she provokes me."

"That's all I needed to know to make sure I never get on your bad side," Denise said seriously.

"Somehow, I think it was more than that, so why don't we give them a moment?" Savannah suggested, nodding towards Denise to follow her lead.

I'd expected some type of smartass comment once we were alone, but it was apparent that she was taking my threat to shoot her seriously.

"We need to talk," I said, moving to the foot of the bed she was laying in.

"So talk."

"I've gotta leave for a day or two and while I'm gone, I expect you to do the right thing. I know that's asking a lot of you, but the Amanda I know wouldn't keep her daughter away from her father."

"You know as well as I do that her father ain't the average muthafucka one gets pregnant by, so desperate measures were necessary to protect my child," she replied.

"You know Dollar would never hurt his child, so don't come with that bullshit."

"But, what if she wasn't his child? I know you're not naïve enough to believe Dollar has a conscience that allows him to spare children from death. When I first got pregnant, I really didn't know who Kyla's father was. True enough, I was only fucking one dude on the side and we used a condom every time, but nothing is one hundred percent, except not having sex. There was no way I could've gone to Dollar and told him the truth, and the fact that he shot me proves I was right," she said.

The love I had for my husband made me want to argue with her logic, but I remembered all too well the way he'd blown my ex-boyfriend away, and the infant he'd been holding. Dollar didn't necessarily believe in good, bad, right, or wrong in the traditional way most people did, and I knew that made him capable of anything. He didn't battle with his demons. He simply became more evil than anything he faced. Even knowing that, I still felt like he would've spared Amanda's life had he known the truth, and he definitely would've been there for his daughter.

"Tell me the story," I demanded.

"I'll give you the highlights. I met him in New York, and it was only supposed to be about sex, but we fell for each other. He never lied about who and what he was, but he didn't keep it one hundred at first. His friend, Fingers, told me the truth about the man I loved and—"

"Wait, you cheated on Dollar with a nigga named Fingers?" I asked, fighting to suppress my laughter.

"Your judgement is not needed because I regretted that decision for a long time after it was over. Now, shut up and listen."

I put my hands in the air, closing my mouth and giving her my undivided attention.

"Anyway, everything was good between Dollar and me, but I fucked up and got high one night. Fingers was the one I got the crack from, and we both knew what would happen if Dollar ever found out. Something about sharing one secret inspires you to share more, and me having sex with Fingers turned into our dirty little secret. I knew I was fucked up for what I was doing, but getting high was more important than doing the right thing. I never knew how Dollar found out, maybe it was because him and Fingers were that close, or maybe we'd simply gotten sloppy. Either way, Dollar found out and kicked in the door to the motel room we'd been in that day. We weren't fucking when he ran down on us, but I could tell by the look on Dollar's face that it didn't matter, because I'd still made the mistake of betraying him. He shot out Fingers's kneecaps so he couldn't run, and then shot me in the throat. He thought I was dead because I'd fallen on the other side of the bed, and I wasn't dumb enough to correct his misconception. I was lucky that someone had heard the shots, and that the paramedics' response time was world-record fast. It was discovered while they were saving my life in the hospital that I was pregnant, and I knew I had to disappear. I did, and managed to stay off any radar that would bring me into contact with Dollar. Never in my wildest dreams did I think that you would show up with him on your arm."

After hearing her side of the story, her response to seeing Dollar now made perfect sense. If she'd had a gun, she undoubtedly would've shot him without hesitation, and knowing that had me questioning the wisdom in my decision to leave them under the same roof. There was more than history and bad blood between them though, and that's what I needed them to understand.

"Amanda, I love you and—"

"If you love me, then call me Katie. I know you don't like that name because of our father, but I used the name Amanda when I was turning tricks. That part of my life is over."

"Fair enough. Katie, I love you, and I love Dollar. I get why you did what you did, but that's all in the past now. You may think he's a monster, but I know my man and the moment you told him the truth about Kyla, he forgave you for the past. He can talk all the shit he wants about not forgiving, but I know what he values in this world. A child of his is at the top of that list," I said.

"Apparently so, since he's kept his other daughter a secret from the world."

"Okay, first of all, Iree is not his daughter in the traditional sense. She's his little sister, but since their dad died a long time ago, Dollar has been there for her. He loves her like his daughter, and he'd do anything in the world for her, just like she would for him. Their relationship is as complicated as it is beautiful, but seeing how he is with her makes me want to have his baby," I confessed.

"Wow! That's saying a lot because the last time I checked, you were done with diapers and bottle feedings."

"I threw any plan I'd made for my life out the window once I met Dollar, and I have no regrets. That man is amazing and I love him. He'd be an amazing father to Kyla too."

I could tell by the indecision on her face that she was actually considering what I was saying. I didn't know that I could ask much more of her than that right now.

"This shit is just so crazy!" she said, shaking her head.

"Believe me, I still ain't got over the disbelief of all of this, but I know it'll make a hell of a story one day."

"Yeah, but who are we gonna tell? Nobody would believe this shit and if they did, Dollar would shut them up permanently," she replied, chuckling softly.

I couldn't help laughing with her because she was right. Dollar was not the type to advertise his business, especially not his personal business.

"Listen, sis, you know I love you and I would never put my niece in any type of danger. Just talk to Dollar and come to a mature, adult compromise because you would rather do that than have him force you to do shit his way. You know like I do he can and will do some shit like that, and I'd rather avoid all the unnecessary drama. Wouldn't you?" I asked seriously.

"I mean, I guess. I just don't understand what you expect to come from this."

"Harmony, that's all I want. I'll call you to check on you later," I replied, standing up and moving over to her so I could kiss her on the cheek.

"Are you really not gonna apologize for shooting me, bitch?"

"Nah, you deserved it."

I could hear her cursing me out the whole time I was walking down the hallway, but I just laughed while tucking my pistol and kept moving. I made it downstairs and outside, where I found Rain and Iree engaged in a sensual lip boxing match, and it was obvious they didn't care who saw them.

"Are you seriously trying to give your grandparents a heart attack, Rain?" I asked, looking around to see if my parents were outside.

Thankfully, they were oblivious to what was going on behind them because they were talking to Dollar down by their car. I let them continue saying goodbye in their own way, until I caught sight of their hands trying to get in on the action.

"Iree, don't make me shoot you," I warned.

This comment made them pull back reluctantly, but the look Iree turned on me said that she was contemplating trying me.

"It's not a good idea, I promise. And no matter what she says to provoke you, I need you to not get into no shit with our guest. If you can do that, I'll make sure that you living here permanently ain't an issue."

"So, you are staying here?" Rain asked Iree.

"That's the plan. Will you come visit me when you're not in school?"

Both girls turned to me to get my response to this question, although I hadn't been asked it. The truth was that I wanted both of my kids to stay here with me, Dollar, and Iree on a permanent basis, but we had to sort through some of the chaos first.

"Do you wanna come back for Thanksgiving in a few weeks?" I asked Rain.

"Thank you, Mommy!"

I would've told her she was welcome, but she launched herself at me and hugged me hard enough to knock the wind out of me. The next thing I knew, Iree was hugging me.

"O-okay you two. Rain, we gotta go, so say a quick goodbye and meet me at the car."

By the time they let me go and I made it down the stairs, Dollar was waiting for me a few feet away from my parents' car.

"I thought I was gonna have to come up there and separate you from Katie, or clean up the mess you'd made."

"No need, I left her in one piece and gave her a lot to think about," I replied, stepping into his open arms.

"Oh yeah? Do I even want to know the conversation you had with her?"

"She told me about you two," I said honestly.

The cloud that came over his face appeared quicker than an unexpected tornado and it was just as surprising, because it came with something I knew was completely foreign to him. Guilt.

"I'm not one to regret shit, you knew that, but if I would've known about the baby—"

"I know, bae, and I told my sister that. She may not believe me one hundred percent, but if you talk to her and show her you're capable of forgiving her past, maybe she'll forgive you for yours."

Despite how serious this topic of discussion was, I couldn't help but notice how cute he looked when his emotions were at war. I was positive I was the only one who got to see him like this, and I loved it. I pulled him towards me, and kissed him passionately enough to let him know I really didn't wanna leave his side.

"Nice way to be a hypocrite, Mom," Rain said from behind me.

Her words didn't stop my tongue from conversing intimately with his, nor did they stop my panties from being sucked in by my pussy lips. The only thing that made me unlock my lips from his were the warning bells sounding off in my head. I'd had enough experience with the sexual chemistry we created to know that if I didn't stop, my panties would be off quicker than a starter's pistol, and the fucking would be on.

"I'll be back in a couple days," I whispered against his lips.

"Hurry."

When he shoved the key to his Ferrari in my hand, I knew just how serious he was about me getting back here quick, fast, and in a hurry.

"I love you. Try not to kill you know who."

"No promises," he replied, smiling in a serious way.

"Ray-Ray, you're riding with me," I said, turning and going to the driver's side of the Ferrari.

"Cool!"

"That's not fair, Mom, I'm older," Rain protested.

"You've already gone for a joy ride, so let your little brother have some fun," I replied, climbing behind the wheel.

She stood outside my parents' Buick station wagon for a few moments pouting, but once she saw that Ray-Ray wasn't giving up his seat, she climbed in the car and we got on the move.

"Mom, what do you call a fish with two knees?"

"I don't know, Ray, what?"

"A tunee fish," he replied, cracking up with laughter.

Telling each other corny jokes was our own special thing, our way of bonding and sharing the love that we had for each other. We'd been doing it for years and I cherished every moment, because I feared he'd outgrow it as he got older.

"Why don't shoe strings ever win a race?" I asked.

"I don't know, why?"

"Because they always tie!" I replied, laughing with him.

We spent the entire drive to Alabama telling jokes and laughing until we were in tears, but I could tell as we got closer to my parents' house, he had something serious on his heart.

"What's on your mind, fat daddy?" I asked.

"A lot of stuff."

"Well, Ray, you know you can talk to me about anything, so what's up?"

He hesitated for a few more moments, but I didn't mind waiting to hear whatever he needed to say to me.

"How long will it be before I see you again?" he asked.

"Well, that depends. Do you like my new house?"

"Mmm-hmm."

"And what about Dollar, do you like him?" I asked cautiously.

"Yeah, Dollar is cool. He loves you a lot."

I couldn't stop the grin that crept over my face at hearing my son's words. Kids moved off of instincts that weren't even honed yet, allowing them to analyze things with a purity that was based on black and white, which cut out the bullshit that came with gray areas. I didn't doubt my husband's love, but my little man being able to see it, only proved it was as real as a rainbow in the sky.

"Yeah, he does love me, and we're gonna be together forever. That means you can come to our house whenever you want. So to answer your question, you can see me when you want, as long as it doesn't interfere with your school."

"Deal," he replied, quickly sticking his hand out for me to shake.

"Nice doing business with you. Now, how about we get some ice cream before I take you home?"

"Onward!" he said, dramatically pointing towards the windshield.

He kept me laughing all the way to Baskin Robbins, and onward to my parents' house, but when I pulled up in front of their house, the smile on my face vanished.

"Ray-Ray, I need you to stay in the car, and don't get out until I tell you to. Understand?"

The sight of me pulling out my gun and slowly chambering a round had his tongue stuck in his mouth, but I saw him nod his head in the darkness. I had no idea what I was walking into, but the sight of two men holding my parents, while one pointed a gun at Rain meant I had to act regardless. I slowly pushed the car door open and stepped out. With the speed and stealth of a ninja I managed to get within a few feet of the muthafucka holding the gun, but he never got the chance to know it. With two quick pulls of the trigger, I made his head explode all over my dad's back.

"Think about it," I warned the second man, halting his reaching motion. "Who are you and what do you want?" I asked.

"We're just here for you, Tabitha. If you go with me quietly, your family won't be harmed."

"Let my mother go," I said, as if I were actually negotiating.

As soon as he did that, my mom ran into my dad's arms.

"Before we go, tell me who sent you," I demanded.

"I worked for the man your sister murdered, and now I work for his wife. Your sister stole a lot of money and now that she's out, we're gonna need that back."

"So, are you saying if I give you my sister, you'll leave me and my family alone?" I asked calmly.

"Yes."

His answer made my decision easy. I shot him twice in the chest and then advanced on his fallen body.

"Tabitha, don't!" my mother said, when I leaned down and put the gun to his forehead.

I glanced at her briefly before turning back to him and grinning.

"That good Christian woman right there just saved your soul, and I think you should thank her," I said seriously.

"Th-thank—"

That was as far as he got before I pulled the trigger and made his brains part of the lawn's fertilizer.

"Take Dad and the kids, and leave. Drive west and don't stop until you get to Texas."

"Tab—"

"I love you, Mom, but you've gotta go. Now."

Aryanna

Chapter 5
Dollar

"What you doing, Dad?"

"Day dreaming," I replied honestly, looking away from the laptop's screen to where Iree stood.

"I figured you could use this."

She walked into my office and passed me a lit blunt. I could tell by the glassy look in her eyes that she was already walking on the clouds.

"You're getting way too comfortable with my weed stash, using the excuse of bringing me a blunt as a reason to smoke one yourself," I said, hitting the blunt hard.

"First of all, it's your wife's weed and she doesn't care how much I smoke, so you can shut that petty shit up. More importantly, I bring you blunts because I'm a considerate and thoughtful daughter, who understands you've got a lot going on right now."

I smiled at her response while continuing to smoke.

"I'll just say thank you, and leave it at that. What are you doing up this late anyway, you missing Rain already?"

"It's crazy because I could've sworn it was just sex, but it was hella hard to say goodbye to her earlier," she admitted, sitting down in the seat across from me.

"Shit sneaks up on you, don't it? One minute you're just fucking and the next minute, you're married."

"Are you talking about you and Honey, or you and her sister?" she asked, smiling.

That question required a couple more healthy pulls on the blunt before passing it to her, and contemplating thoughtfully.

"My marriage to Honey was about two halves becoming a whole. I've never felt as complete with anyone, or as

49

relaxed, so I know our union is about all the right things in the world. Katie, well, my marriage to her was different."

"Did you love her?" Iree asked softly, passing me the blunt back.

Did I love her? Was there an easy answer to that question?

"I loved her in a way I didn't think possible, simply because I actually trusted her. When she betrayed that trust, I doubted I'd ever love anyone again, but I've never been so glad to be wrong about anything," I confessed.

"She betrayed you. So, what happened after that, because I doubt you'd let any bitch just take your kid and vanish. All I ever knew was that you went through a rough divorce."

"You could say that, and that is what I told your mom. The truth is I killed her, or at least I thought I did. I shot her, but I never knew she was pregnant though. Had I known..."

I let that thought go because there was no telling how different my life would be. It hurt to know I had a daughter who was a complete mystery to me, but there was no way for me to imagine my life without Honey in it.

"How old is your daughter?" she asked.

"Two and a half, I think. I don't know anything about her."

"You and I have had our differences, but when it comes to having you in my life as a father, I'll always love you and be grateful. I don't want your daughter to miss out on all the love you have to give, so give me that blunt and go upstairs so you can talk with your baby mama."

"It's too late for that, she's gotta be sleep at two a.m.," I replied.

"Speaking from the experience of recently being shot in my leg, I'm almost positive she's awake. Every time she moves, she feels pain."

Having been shot not too long ago my damn self, I knew how true her statement was, but I was still hesitant to talk to Katie. I did wanna know about our daughter though.

"I can see you arguing with yourself, so I'ma help you out. Stop being a bitch, get up, and go handle your muthafuckin' business," she instructed, holding her hand out for the blunt.

I blew smoke in her face out of spite, while refusing to give her my blunt as I left the room and headed upstairs. Her laughter trailed after me. I knew my approach to Katie's room had been made with minimal noise, but as soon as I got to the door, I found her eyes locked on my location.

"You okay?" I asked softly.

"No. I'm hoping you came to finish me off, because my leg hurts like a muthafucka."

"Yeah, Iree warned me that you might be awake and in pain."

"What the hell would she know about this pain?" Katie asked, gritting her teeth as she sat up against the head board.

"Trust me, she knows, her own bullet wound is still healing."

"She-she got shot?" Katie asked in disbelief.

"Yeah, but she deserved it."

"That's the same bullshit my sister said about me, but I know you wouldn't let her shoot your daughter."

"No, I shot her," I confessed.

I could tell my admission left her speechless, and I immediately regretted my honestly, considering the topic I'd come to discuss with her.

"You want some?" I asked, crossing the room to her bed and holding the blunt out.

"I can't, I'm a recovering addict. I couldn't even take the pain medication your doctor tried to give me earlier."

"I can understand pain pills, but this is just bud. I ain't never heard of nobody overdosing off of marijuana because if it were possible, I'd incorporate it into my bag of tricks," I replied, smiling.

She shook her head, but I caught the ghost of a smile cross her face. After another moment of hesitation, she extended her hand and accepted the blunt.

"If I relapse, I'm blaming you," she said.

"You're strong enough to fight against the urge to relapse."

My statement froze her movement for a second as she stared at me, but she quickly shook it off and hit the blunt. I couldn't help laughing at her when she started choking, even though I knew that was gonna make her hit it harder the next time. I waved her off when she tried to pass it back, and took a seat beside her on the bed. I wasn't sure how to start the conversation I wanted to have, so I chose to wait her out.

"I know you didn't come up here to bring me a blunt and sit with me in the middle of the night, Dollar, so what's up?"

"Kyla."

Speaking my daughter's name was like pointing directly at the purple elephant standing in the middle of the room, but there was really no sense in beating around the bush.

"What do you wanna know?" she asked, exhaling heavily.

"Everything, anything, I don't know. Just tell me something about her."

"She has both of our independent personalities, but she's got your mean streak. She's smart, especially for only being two and a half years old, and sometimes that translates into her being a smart ass."

"Definitely your DNA in her," I said, smiling.

"Guilty. She's amazing though, and it's impossible not to love her. The last time I saw her, she was a chunky little thing, but I heard she's getting taller and slimmer already."

"Where is she, Katie?"

This question caused her to put the blunt back in between her lips and hit it hard. Even in the moonlight I could see the indecision clouding her brown eyes, but I didn't press her. Not yet anyway.

"We need to talk more before I answer that," she replied.

"Fair enough. What do you want to talk about?"

"Well, you could always start by apologizing for trying to kill me," she said.

If she hadn't been smiling when she said this, I might've cussed her ass out, but I decided to do the unthinkable.

"I'm sorry, Katie."

Her smirk vanished, leaving her mouth hanging open in shock. I calmly reached over and closed it for her.

"You just, you just apologized."

"I know, I was right here when I did it," I replied, chuckling.

"But, you don't, you don't need to apologize, Dollar. Not for anything!"

"Yeah, well, I've learned over the years that not even I can be right at all times. In this instance, me making the wrong decision has cost me two and a half years of my daughter's life."

I thought her mouth was gonna fall open again, but instead she just kept looking at me like I had three heads.

"Wow. Okay, well, I'm sorry about the whole situation with Fingers. I was fucked up for ever dealing with him, it was just—"

"We don't have to talk about that. I got all those answers from Fingers," I said.

"Of course you did. I'm still sorry because you didn't deserve that."

"It may be hard for you to believe, but I understand what it's like to be addicted to something and being powerless to stop or leave it alone," I confessed.

We both knew I was talking about killing so there was no need to further elaborate., She was shocked by how our conversation had gone so far, I could tell that even through the weed fog that was quickly swarming her. I was just hoping this would help her understand that I wanted to do things differently. Her sudden laughter had me looking at her with concern.

"You good?" I asked.

"I'm high as fuck, but I'm good. I was thinking about some of the funny shit that your daughter does."

"Tell me about it," I said.

She patted the spot on the bed next to her, and I lay beside her. The trip down memory lane started with Kyla as an infant, and by the time the sun was due to rise, I couldn't remember ever laughing so hard in my entire life.

"Sounds like she does have equal parts of our personalities," I said.

"That she does, but I wouldn't change anything about her."

"Not even who her father is?" I asked casually.

I didn't remember her lying down, but I felt when she turned her head to look at me. I couldn't read her expression entirely. I just knew it wasn't as openly hostile as it had been recently.

"Our daughter was created in love, Dollar. I never loved Fingers, and sex was nothing more than an exchange of goods. I swear to you on Kyla's life that I loved you, and that's why we made her."

I didn't really know how to respond to that, but before I could, her lips were suddenly on mine. If anybody would've asked me, I would've put my life on my desire to have a gun in my mouth, followed closely by a bullet, than to have Katie's tongue exploring the space behind my lips. So then why was I kissing her back? Why was I not smacking her hand away as her fingers worked my zipper and pulled my dick out? Why was I ignoring the screaming going on in my mind, instead of enjoying the taste of weed on her tongue? I couldn't answer even one of those questions, and the way she was stroking my dick made it clear that she had no intention of asking me a damn thing.

"Your leg," I said, stopping her from pulling me on top of her.

"We'll make it work. Come here."

It had been years since I heard that hunger in her voice, but it was easily recognizable, and as familiar as some old bedroom slippers. She spread her thick thighs wide in welcome, pulling her panties aside so that there was nothing guarding the devil's gateway to pleasure. Common sense told me not to stick my dick inside her, but before I knew it, I was pushing steadily past her pussy lips and fighting with the current of her wetness.

"W-wait a second," she said.

"Is, it your leg, because—"

"No, it's-it's just been awhile so I n-need to adjust," she replied, closing her eyes and taking a deep breath.

A few seconds later, her eyes popped open and it was like the woman beneath me had stepped out of a time machine. I felt her squeezing her pussy muscles as she pulled my mouth back to hers, and that was the only signal I needed to move. My strokes were slow, but they didn't lack power and within moments, I could hear the familiar growl in her throat. The combination of moisture and heat inside her made her feel like an exotic rainforest, and it was completely intoxicating. The faster I moved, the higher she took me, until I felt like I was looking down at the world through God's eyes.

"Don't-don't cum in me," she panted.

"I w-won't."

As the sun rose around us, I got a clear look at her eyes, and even though I saw tears clouding her vision, the need she felt was unmistakable. I fed her dick at a steady rhythm, muffling the sounds of passion leaping from her throat with possessive kisses, until she came with the force of a nuclear explosion. I thought I could hang on and keep going, but her pussy's grip was firmer than any handshake, and she squeezed my climax out of me. It wasn't until our bodies had stopped trembling that I realized what I'd inadvertently done.

"Why, Dollar?"

"I didn't-I didn't mean to, I just got caught up in the moment," I replied lamely.

She sucked her teeth in obvious annoyance, while pushing on my chest so I would get off her. I understood why cumming in her was a bad idea, but it really had been unintentional. The last thing I needed was for her to get pregnant. I knew she felt the same way, but I thought she was being a little dramatic by rolling over and turning her back to me. That move made it clear she wanted to be left alone, so I climbed out of the bed with the intentions of doing just that. I was trying to wrap my mind around what the fuck I'd just done and what it meant, but when I stepped foot in the hallway, my thoughts took a different turn. Standing a few feet away, with both of her hands clamped over her mouth was Iree, and it was clear by the expression on her face that she knew something she shouldn't. I didn't say a word, I simply motioned for her nosy ass to go back downstairs and I followed her lead.

"Outside," I said when she turned in the direction of my office.

Once we got out there, we fell into step together, heading towards the creek.

"What were you doing?" I asked.

"Uh-un, don't start fishing with that lame ass question because I know what you were doing."

"I don't know what you think happened, but—"

"Dollar, I love you to death and you know that, but you're caught, bruh. I didn't have to physically see you with your dick in her to know that you were fucking and FYI, there's no such thing as cumming quietly, unless you're alone masturbating."

"Okay, so we had sex," I said nonchalantly.

"Oooh, then it's worse than I thought. If you would've just fucked her, then it could've been forgotten, but you said you had sex, and that means emotion was involved on some level."

"You really think I'm about to listen to the psycho-analyzing of a sixteen-year-old?"

"You ain't got to, but we both know I know a thing or two about sexual relations," she pointed out.

All I could do was shake my head and keep walking. Her soft laughter wasn't helping matters, but I was suddenly distracted by the sound of a car approaching. I stopped and turned, feeling a sudden unease at the sight of Honey's parents' station wagon coming to a stop in front of my house. That unease morphed into something closer to fear when I looked back up the driveway and didn't see my Ferrari in the distance.

"Ain't that—"

"Yeah, it is," I replied, heading towards their car at a fast walk.

"Where's Honey?" I asked before anyone could step out of the car.

"I don't know," her mother replied.

The look on her face was one of pain, but before I could hit her over the head with follow-up questions, the back door of the car opened and Ray-Ray hit the ground at a dead sprint. Within seconds he'd catapulted his little body into mine, forcing me to catch him or have us both hit the ground.

"You ok, big guy?" I asked, holding him close.

He didn't say anything, but I could feel his body trembling as he cried, and that brought my fear to life.

"You and your husband meet me in my office," I said, turning around and taking Ray-Ray in the house. I took him to my game room and once he'd calmed down, I left him in the capable clutches of the gaming world. I could see Rain and Iree through the screen door talking softly on the porch, and the look on Rain's face told a story of something bad happening.

"What happened?" I asked, as soon as I entered my office.

Mr. Dewhitt simply shook his head, which left it up to his wife to fill me in. Once she'd done that, I calmly took the all-black Ruger .380 I kept in my desk drawer, and walked up the stairs to Katie's room.

"I need you to tell me everything about the man you killed."

At first, she didn't even turn over, but the sound of me chambering a round into my pistol made her look at me quickly.

"Wh-why Dollar, what's wrong?"

"No questions right now, just tell me everything about him. Quickly."

Aryanna

Chapter 6
Honey
Tennessee
Two days later

"Well, look who's slumming and decided to grace us with her presence."

"Don't be an asshole, Seth," I said, pushing past his short stocky frame, and stepping in his trailer.

I couldn't remember the last time I'd been here, but from the looks of things, shit had only gone downhill.

"How can you live in such filth?" I asked, disgusted by the smell of old grease, older food, and stale air.

"You can take your high-sadity ass, right back to whatever rock you crawled from under if you don't like my living arrangements, because I don't remember inviting you anyway!"

I bit back my response because the overflowing ashtrays, empty food containers, and trash on the floor weren't my concern or reason for being here. One thing I knew for sure was that only love could make me step into this part of the past.

"Where's my niece?" I asked.

For some reason, the sound of his laughter as he crossed the room and glopped down in his recliner made me want to shoot him in the face. I resisted the urge, but damn, was it hard.

"What's funny about that question, Seth?"

"It's funny that you show up here and ask about my niece like you're actually worried about her. Kyla has seen you twice since she was born, and now you're here out of the blue. Why?"

The last thing I wanted to do was explain myself to this beady eyed muthafucka, but the curious look on his face indicated I'd have to do just that. I took a deep breath to steady my rolling stomach, knowing I only wanted to vomit because of the resemblance Seth had to my late sperm donor. It was uncanny really, because even though Seth was Katie's brother, they only shared the same mother, not father. At least, that was the story. Right now, I was questioning that but it didn't matter, because nothing would make me consider him my brother.

"I don't have time for your shit, Seth. I'm here about Kyla because Katie wants her. So, where is she?"

"Are they starting up a daycare center in prison now? I didn't see that on the news," he replied, laughing as he lit a cigarette.

"You're funny, but no. Our dear sister is once again a free woman, and she wants to get on with her life which includes her daughter. So, I'll ask you again, where is Kyla?"

"She's not here," he replied vaguely.

The bastard was trying my patience, and the fact that he was doing it with a smile on his face only made it worse. Before I lost all my patience, I decided to look around the trailer and see if he was completely full of shit. It only took a couple minutes to search the tiny space, and I didn't find Kyla, but what disturbed me was that I didn't find any trace of her. No kid's clothes, no toys, nothing to indicate that a child lived here. That gave me a bad feeling.

"I'm done fucking around with you, Seth, where the fuck is Kyla?"

"Your concern is touching, really it is, but you're from the streets, so you know that information don't come cheap."

His statement only increased the bad feeling that I had, because it sounded like wherever Kyla was, he wasn't expecting her back anytime soon. It was becoming clear to me this was now a situation I needed to handle with finesse.

"The fact that you're gonna charge me just to tell me our niece is at a sleepover is crazy, but I can understand if you're hard pressed for money. How much?" I asked.

"Oh, I'm hard alright, but it's not for money. Besides, that piece of shit Toyota Corolla you pulled up in means your pockets are holding lint just like mine. Your pussy probably has the same amount of miles as that car, but it definitely has more value."

I wondered, if he knew about my husband's Ferrari that I'd stashed before stealing the bucket out front, would he feel the same way? The odds were that he would because he always looked at me a little too hard. It didn't matter that we shared a sister because we didn't share DNA, but then again, that probably wouldn't have mattered to this Tennessee hillbilly either. Without a doubt he would stick his dick in anything and anyone. Just not me though.

"Let me get this straight, you wanna fuck me in exchange for telling me where Kyla is? What type of twisted shit is that?"

"You can call it twisted all you like, Tabitha, but I know you, and I know that you've wanted some of this for years."

To demonstrate his belief he stood up, unzipped his pants, and pulled his penis out. I knew instinctively that if I laughed, I'd more than likely have to kill him right here but honestly, there was no way that he hadn't been laughed at before with that penis.

"You do know that there's a difference between dick and penis, right?" I asked.

"Huh?"

I could tell by the dumb look on his face that the insult I'd shot at him had gone straight over his head, but I wasn't surprised. Any muthafucka who thought pulling out something that was barely four inches on hard was enticing to a woman, was obviously way past stupid.

"Alright, look, if we're doing this then we need to make it quick, because I've got shit to do," I said, pulling my t-shirt over my head.

Of course, I wasn't wearing a bra because Dollar liked to randomly suck my titties throughout the day, and the sight of my powder pink nipples had Seth hypnotized.

"Don't just stand there, fool, go clean off that bed in the back, and let's do this."

The sound of my voice broke his trance, and had him scrambling to put his cigarette out before he dashed to the back of the trailer.

"And get those clothes off!" I yelled after him.

Once I heard him fumbling around, I quickly went to the kitchen and grabbed the biggest knife I could find. I would've really preferred to shoot him, but I had no doubt that his neighbors were close enough to hear a loud fart, so a gunshot would sound off like cannon fire. I stripped off the rest of my clothes before walking back to his room with both hands behind my back. I knew this wouldn't alarm him since this allowed for my titties to sit up even higher, and command his undivided attention.

"On the bed," I demanded.

"Should-should I put the condom on or do you wanna do that?"

"Have at it, champ, I'll just enjoy watching you," I replied, moving to the foot of the bed.

When he grabbed a gold wrapper out of his nightstand, I doubted my ability to keep a straight face, but when he actually lay down and tried to put the Magnum on, I couldn't take it.

"That's like putting a human raincoat on a poodle," I said, laughing hysterically.

"Funny, bitch, just get up here on top of me."

The anger on his face only made me laugh harder, until I could feel the tears rolling down my face.

"Since it's so damn funny, I'll be sure to put it in your asshole too, and then in your mouth without washing it," he declared.

I was still chuckling when I climbed on the bed, but both of our expressions changed to deadly serious at the same time.

"The coldness that you feel is not my hand, it's the cool steel of a knife against your shaft, and you know what this thing is," I said, waving at him with the gun in my other hand.

"T-Tabitha, please—"

"Nope, you don't get to beg, at least not yet. You do get to tell me where the fuck Kyla is, and you better be smart enough to know the consequences for lying."

"She-she's gone, she doesn't live here anymore," he replied shakily.

In all the conversations Katie and I'd had while she was locked up over the last year, she'd told me that Kyla was with her brother, Seth. Never had there been any mention of her moving or going to live with someone else, which meant Seth was either full of shit, or my sister had no idea where her own daughter was.

"Ah!" he shrieked, feeling the serrated blade slice cleanly through the condom.

"I'm so not fucking with you, Seth, which means you better explain what happened quickly."

"Okay-okay, I will. Six months ago, a man came to me and said he represented the man Katie had killed. He said the man Katie killed was actually Kyla's dad, and the family was now prepared to provide for Kyla for the rest of her life."

"And you actually believed that shit?" I asked, tasting the rage on my tongue.

"Yeah, I mean, he showed up and handed me fifty thousand dollars in cash, so I figured he was on the level."

"No, you believed the cash was on the level, you piece of shit," I growled, moving the knife again.

"I swear-I swear I had no reason not to believe him! Nobody wants to raise a kid that ain't theirs."

"The flaw in your logic is that the man Katie killed was white, and any fucking idiot with eyes can see Kyla is mixed with black!"

I expected him to kick some type of half-assed logic or justification out of his mouth, but I witnessed something even worse. I watched as that realization dawned on him with the weight of a concept never heard before. Whoever those people were had bet on money stopping any logical question Seth might've had, and they'd been right.

"Where did the man take Kyla?"

"I-I don't know," he replied fearfully.

I hated to admit it, but I actually fucking believed him. Leaning forward, I put the gun to his head and the knife to his throat.

"What did this man look like?"

"Br-broad shoulders, white, brown hair, nice s-suit," he stammered.

Just based on the description he gave, I knew looking for that man would be pointless, because he was on ice in an Alabama morgue by now.

"Give me a name or some information to save your miserable life."

"I-I don't know anything else, Tabitha, please—"

His begging was suddenly lost in the sound of him gurgling his own blood from the gash I'd put in his throat. The way his blood misted all over my face and neck didn't make me move off of him, because I was determined to watch his life reach its conclusion. His body spasmed and twitched hard enough to buck me off him, but I rode him into the afterlife. It just wasn't how he'd envisioned it. Once his body went still and his eyes were forever looking through me, I climbed off of him and went to the bathroom. I'd feared it wouldn't be any more sanitary than any other part of the trailer and I was right, but I still had to take a shower. I did it as quick as possible, wiped my prints off the knife after washing it, get dressed, and left as quickly as I'd come. I managed to make it to the supermarket parking lot a few miles away without being pulled over, and I quickly wiped the car down before getting out and sliding back behind the wheel of the Ferrari. Once I was back on the move, I contemplated what my next move should be. Common sense said I had no business in Tennessee after killing two people here a few days ago, but as far as I knew, the cops weren't looking for me. I'd made sure to check before crossing state lines, because I wasn't about to hear Dollar's mouth if he had to break me out of prison. That didn't mean I necessarily felt comfortable moving around out here, so I needed to get Kyla and get the fuck back to Mississippi fast. My instincts to come this far had been right, because I figured whoever was after my sister wouldn't be satisfied with simply coming after me to get to her. Naively, I'd thought they'd started with me, but it was obvious the play to get Katie was one that had been thought out and planned. What they hadn't planned on was me and Dollar, which meant they weren't aware that they'd just pissed off the devil and his wife. God fearing we might be, but neither of us hesitated when it came to bringing hell to Earth. I'd never known a man that could tap into that side of me while still keeping me under control. Indulging in my savage side had always been an exercise in all or nothing, but my husband balanced me out. I wanted desperately to call him, but I knew he needed to deal with Katie and all that drama. There would be no way for him to do that if he was on the hunt, so like the female lion, I would hunt and bring the kill home to my king. I just needed to figure out the best way to stalk my prey.

A sign I drove past suddenly gave me an idea, allowing me to put my foot down harder on the gas as my destination crystalized in my mind. Twenty minutes later, I pulled up outside of a strip club called, Shake Your Ass. Being unsure of what security measures I would encounter, forced me to put my gun under the driver's seat before I stepped out and made my way inside. The dueling smells of men's body spray and women's perfume assaulted my nostrils as soon as I opened the door, but they still didn't cover up the funk of sweat and used pussy. It took a few seconds for my eyes to adjust to the dim lighting, but once I could see I made my way over to a table and sat down.

"There's a two-drink minimum, what can I get you?" a short, petite blonde asked.

Her titties were so big that I didn't know how she was standing up, but she was cute.

"I'll have a rum and Coke, and a dance from you," I replied, pulling out a twenty-dollar-bill and passing it to her.

"No problem, sweetie, I'll be right back."

I admired the sway of her hips and the jiggle of her ass cheeks as she walked away and hoped she smelled as good as she looked, because the last thing I wanted to inhale was funky pussy. While I waited, my eyes scanned the club, taking in the limited customers and shabby décor, but searching for something more important. I'd never been in this particular spot, but to my knowledge, all strip clubs were more or less the same.

"Here you go, sweetie."

I accepted my drink before leaning back in my seat so I could enjoy the show.

"What's your name?" I asked.

"Dreamer."

"I like that, it's not typical for this profession," I said, sipping my drink.

"You'll find that I'm not typical."

The twinkle in her blue eyes when she said that made my pussy twitch, but I just smiled and continued to stare at her. Her dance started off slow, sensual in technique and the intimacy she created with subtle movements of her limber body. To my delight, she smelled like fresh oranges when she straddled me and shoved her titties in my face.

"Be careful with those things," I said, smiling.

"I'm sure you can handle them," she replied seductively, pushing her nipple to within inches of my mouth.

The challenge in her eyes was as blatant as it was beautiful. When my tongue shot from between my lips, and skated across the taut pink flesh of her nipple, that challenge quickly changed to shock and desire.

"I get the feeling you're quite skilled with your tongue," she whispered.

"You have no idea."

"Now coming to the main stage, April Showers!" a hidden voice announced.

Hearing this turned my head to the stage a few feet away, and I smiled at the sight of my sister from another mister strutting out. April Showers was really a girl named Ashley that I'd done a little time with once upon a time in my checkered past. She was beautiful, standing six feet, weighing a well-portioned two hundred and twenty pounds, with natural blonde hair and gorgeous green eyes, but she was more than that beauty. She was a muthafuckin' rider, and that's what I needed.

"I'm about to get off in a few minutes. How about we both get off a little after that?" Dreamer asked, refocusing my attention on her.

"Isn't that supposed to be my line?"

"What can I say, I go for what I want and I'm extremely picky," she replied, smiling at me.

"So am I. Go get your shit."

Without a word, she hopped up off my lap and disappeared through a door. I turned my eyes back to the stage at the exact moment Ashley spotted me.

"Bitch!" she exclaimed excitedly, hopping off stage and rushing towards me.

I barely had time to sit my drink down, before she pulled me out of my seat and into her arms.

"I missed you too," I said, giggling as she squeezed me tight against her.

"What the fuck are you doing here?"

"I came to see you of course, since you never did get around to coming to Florida," I replied.

"Hey, April, get that ass back on stage!" a short, fat guy hollered.

"Hold on, Tab, let me finish my set and—"

"Fuck that set and this place, because you don't gotta work here no more," I said, not letting her go.

"What are you talking about? I need my job."

"Do you trust me, Ash?"

If anyone else had asked her this question she would've been looking at them like they were insane. She came up in the streets like I did, and rule number-one was that trust was something you held onto tighter than your virginity. You could find a man or woman worthy of the pussy, but it was beyond rare to find one worthy of your trust. We'd gone through enough shit for me to feel like I could ask her this question, and that's why she was looking at me curiously.

"You know I trust you."

"Then, let's go," I said, taking her hand and moving towards the door.

"Wait, I gotta get my stuff."

I let her hand go and she disappeared through the same door that Dreamer had. A few minutes later, both woman reappeared and were headed in my direction.

"Do you two know each other?" Ashley asked, pointing at Dreamer.

"No, but we're about to get real acquainted. Come on," I said, leading the way out front.

"Are you riding with me, my car is right there," Dreamer said, pointing at a black Nissan Maxima.

"Where's your ride, Ash?" I asked.

"My boyfriend dropped me off."

"Okay, Dreamer, you follow us," I said, going to the driver side of my car.

"You are not pushing a fucking Ferrari," Ashley said, in disbelief.

"Yeah, it's my husband's."

"Husband?" both women said in unison.

"Don't worry, he's cool with me bumping pussies, so let's go," I replied, getting in.

Everyone followed my lead, and we got on the move.

"Okay bitch, you've got a lot of explaining to do, so start talking," Ashley demanded.

I used the thirty-minute ride to my motel room to give her some of the highlights of my life for the last few months, eventually bringing me to my point for being in Tennessee right now.

"That's crazy," she said, shaking her head for the hundredth time.

"You're telling me, shit, I'm living it. Come on, so I can fuck your friend and send her on her way so we can strategize."

We climbed out of the car and met Dreamer on the sidewalk.

"I'm right here in room one-twelve," I said, pulling out my key card.

I opened the door and led the way inside, feeling for the light switch on the wall. Before I could find it, I felt something hard hit me across the head, and I was suddenly sliding to the floor. I could hear some type of commotion behind me, but the power of the darkness pulling me under was too strong to fight.

Chapter 7
Dollar

"You killed her, I'm telling you."

"For the last goddamn time, I didn't kill her and I'm not about to keep repeating myself, so shut the fuck up," I said in a polite, yet nasty tone.

The way her eyes blazed at me said she wanted to stomp a hole in my heart, but since her nose had just stopped bleeding from the punch I delivered, we both knew she wouldn't try me twice. I'd been gentle the first round by only hitting her ass once in the stomach and once in the face, but if she made me raise my hand to her again, I was gonna ruin her beauty for good. If she was smart, she'd do like her friend sitting beside her, and shut the fuck up. The sound of moaning directed our attention to the bed.

"What-what the hell happened? Which one of you bitches hit me?" Honey asked.

"They didn't hit you, I did," I clarified.

When her eyes swung in my direction, the disorientation vanished like a shadow once the sun moves from behind a cloud.

"Dollar, b-baby, what are you doing here? Why did you hit me? And, why am I tied up to the bed?"

"Which question do you want me to answer first, wife?"

"You're her husband?" the tall blonde asked.

"I am."

"If-if this is about us possibly having sex, I'm sorry. Please don't hurt me," the smaller blonde said.

Her statement caused me to raise an eyebrow at Honey, but all she did was give me a sheepish smile.

"I'm quite aware of my wife's sexual appetite and no, this is not about that. Now, if you sit there quietly, I promise you'll still get an orgasm before you leave."

"From you or her?" she asked, quickly clamping a hand over her mouth.

I chuckled at the mortified expression on her face, and decided to leave her in suspense, while I got back to the matter at hand.

"Sweetheart, I'm here because you've once again gone rogue, and I smacked you over the head with my pistol for the same reason. As for you being tied up, well, that's just fun for me."

"Gone rogue? Baby, how have I gone rogue?" she asked innocently.

"Your mom showed up at the house a couple days ago and told me what happened. Ray-Ray cried in my arms, and Rain is distraught, but instead of being at home comforting them, you're out picking up strippers."

"I prefer the term exotic dancer," the tall blonde said.

"Baby, what's her name?" I asked, pointing with my gun.

"That's Ashley, she's my—"

"It doesn't matter what she is to you. I just need you to explain to her that I will peel the beautiful flesh from her bones and make a quilt to send to her family, if she doesn't stop testing my patience," I said calmly.

"Ash, please chill, because he's dead-ass serious," Honey warned.

Once Ashley nodded her head in understanding, I turned my attention back to Honey.

"Explain yourself," I demanded.

"Well, you already know what happened, but I told my parents to go to Texas, not back to our house."

"And why would you tell them that, when you know that they're more than welcome in our home?"

"Because my sister is there, and I told you what that's like for my mom. Seeing me execute two people already did irreparable damage."

The mention of Katie sent my mind spinning back to our early morning activities from a couple days ago, but thankfully, Ashley's hand shooting straight up in the air distracted me from the guilt. If only momentarily.

"What is it, Ashley?"

"I'm sorry to interrupt but, sis, did you just say what I think you said?"

"Ashley, are you aware that the only good witness is a dead one? And, while my wife may trust you, no one really knows the woman sitting beside you, so you're really putting her life on the line right now."

"Ashley, will you shut up!" the little blonde said, forcefully.

"My sentiments exactly, now back to you, wife. I guess I can understand your logic, but that still doesn't explain why you're out here on your own trying to solve Katie's problems. I know we put family first, but we don't make moves without talking to each other first."

"I know, bae, and I'm sorry. I just thought that your attention needed to be focused on you and Katie coming to an understanding, and the last thing you needed right now was a distraction or an excuse not to do that."

Her words carried the familiar ring of truth, and I never believed she had malicious intent. Smacking her over the head had simply been me trying to knock the sense into her brain, so she'd understand the value of working as a team. Admittedly, it was somewhat of a foreign concept to me, but after almost dying in Chicago, I understood the necessity for change. I moved from my relaxed position against the wall to stand beside Honey.

"I get it, bae, I do. However, you know the penalty," I said, taking aim at her thigh.

"Dollar, don't you fucking shoot me! I'm serious, don't shoot me!"

"It won't kill you, just relax and take a deep breath. Think about the first time you ever had a dick in your asshole, and just breathe through the pain like that."

"You're not fucking funny, Dollar! And you better not shoot me," she said, smiling despite the hint of fear I saw in her eyes.

I knew she wasn't scared of me, but she knew beyond the shadow of a doubt that I'd shoot her, and still love her afterwards.

"Are you saying you're open to compromise?" I asked.

"Yes! Whatever, just don't shoot me!"

"Okay."

I tucked my gun into my jeans and pulled a knife from my pocket.

"You there, little one. What's your name?" I asked.

"D-Dreamer."

"I like that. Okay, Dreamer, I want you to cut my wife's clothes off."

Even after I handed her the knife, the shocked expression remained on her face.

"It's okay, this is the part where I keep my word about you still getting to get a nut," I said, urging her to do as I'd instructed.

"Dollar, we need to talk first, baby, because I—"

"You were under the impression that I wouldn't mind you getting some pussy, and I'm not. I did tell you that you can't have all the fun though, so now we're all gonna enjoy the afternoon together," I said smiling.

"Dollar, listen for a second, bae. I didn't go to the strip club to pick up some out-of-town stranger. I went to get Ashley because I need her help finding Kyla."

The smile instantly left my face and I had no idea what replaced it, but Dreamer suddenly took a step away from me.

"What do you mean, help you find Kyla? Where the fuck is my daughter?"

"Ash, Dreamer, give us a minute and hop in the shower," Honey instructed.

Without any questions or hesitation Ashley grabbed Dreamer by the hand and led her into the bathroom. Once the door was closed, I could hear them talking, but the sound of the shower muffled their voices a few moments later.

"After your family showed up and your mom told me what was going on, I had a conversation with Katie about Kyla's whereabouts, because I knew if you had been targeted then she would be too. Katie said Kyla was safe with her brother, Seth. Are you telling me that she lied to me?"

"Not intentionally, no. She was under the impression that Kyla was with Seth, and you know you and I think on the same wavelength, so that's why I came out here. I just found out the truth like an hour and a half ago."

"Let's hear it," I said, bracing myself mentally.

I listened in silence as she recounted the events that had taken place, and the information she'd gathered. I'd been beyond pissed about her coming out here on her own, especially given her recent indiscretions in this state, but right now I was grateful she'd made her move.

"Katie told me the dude she was accused of killing was her sugar daddy, some rich white man named Eli Datton. Apparently, his name carries some weight around here, which is what almost got her convicted of his killing, except her lawyer was able to prove it was self-defense. Obviously, the family doesn't buy that story, and now they want some payback," I said.

"Most men who like to abuse women are masters at hiding it from everyone, especially those closest to them, so his family probably doesn't believe he was beating on my sister. In their minds, she killed him for no reason and she deserves to rot in prison for that, but seeing as how that's not gonna happen, they're taking matters into their own hands."

"Yeah, well that just got all of them killed, and I do mean all of them. I don't give a fuck what they wanna believe about their precious Eli, because I saw the scars on Katie's back."

"She-she actually showed you those?" Honey asked, surprised.

I nodded my head, thinking about the whip marks that had crisscrossed Katie's flesh. I knew what it was like to wield the power of that whip, and what it did to the person on the receiving end, so I had no doubt that Eli deserved to die for what he'd done. His family choosing not to acknowledge his flaws as a man wasn't my problem, but little did they know they'd just made me their problem. And I wasn't nothing nice.

"What's your plan?" I asked.

"Have Ashley help me find the family that's still local to the Tennessee area and ask them nicely where my step-daughter is—"

Hearing her say she was gonna ask them nicely made me smile down at her with love, because I knew she was my soulmate and counterpart in every sense of the word.

"Okay. While you do that, I'll work on the family that's not local. I'm gonna have to put you into direct contact with

Aubrey, because I can't have you out here working in the blind."

"Oooh, I get to have contact with your infamous sister? Baby, you really do love me, huh?"

"And don't you ever forget it," I replied, leaning down and kissing her tenderly.

I'd secretly feared that after being intimate with Katie my thirst for Honey would be somehow dampened, but I need not have worried. Kissing her now had me craving her more than ever, but I had to handle the business first.

"I'll let Dreamer take care of you while I set things in motion."

"Wait-wait baby, just give me a little something to take the edge off," she replied, smiling seductively.

I spotted the knife that I'd handed Dreamer sitting on the edge of the bed and I grabbed it, after moving my pistol to the back of my jeans I quickly cut her t-shirt off.

"Don't cut my shirts, just pull them off," she said, lifting her hips.

Being that only her hands were restrained by rope to the headboard I was able to do what she wanted, but I did cut her red boy shorts off of her. The way her breathing quickened as I slowly cut straight down the center of the delicate fabric turned me on as much as the hunger I could see swimming in the twin pools of darkening gold watching me. Once I had her bare flesh exposed, I slowly pushed two of my fingers inside her soaking wet pussy, loving the way her beautiful flower opened under my touch.

"B-baby, don't tease me."

"Why not, isn't that what you love the most?" I asked, grinning at her while pushing my fingers deeper.

Her mouth fell open, but no words passed her succulent lips as my thumb found her clit and introduced itself. I continued this slow torture for a few moments, before pulling my fingers out and putting them in my mouth.

"Mmm."

"Dollar, if you l-love me, then put your dick inside me."

I could hear the rising need in her demand, and I could feel the tension in her body screaming for her inner freak to be let out. The motions of me unzipping my jeans, pulling my dick out and climbing in between her juicy thighs were slow and deliberate, only raising the sexual tension level. When I rubbed my dick in between her pussy lips and across her clit, her whole body went stiff, and her lungs ran out of oxygen. Just as I was about to plunge myself inside her, the bathroom door opened beside us and suddenly, we had company.

"Ashley, get dressed, we've gotta take a ride real quick," I said.

"Wait-wait, bae, don't leave me like this!" Honey whined.

I smiled mischievously at her before looking over to the two women standing there, wearing only towels and suspenseful expressions on their faces.

"Dreamer, can you finish what I start?" I asked.

"Absolutely."

"The kid, she got skills," Ashley said, vouching for Dreamer.

"We'll see," I said, turning my attention back to Honey.

I pushed inside her fast and hard, making her eyes roll to the back of her head involuntarily. My second stroke was delivered with the same speed and force, causing her to wrap her legs around my waist to hang on. I pounded her steadily for a few minutes before stopping suddenly, and pulling all the way out of her.

"Dollar, don't!" she exclaimed, trying to keep me locked in between her legs.

"I'll finish you off when I get back," I promised, standing up and chuckling.

The expression on her face was a priceless masterpiece of distress, hunger, and anger.

"That's cold, b-bruh," Ashley said, laughing.

"You're still not dressed yet? Girl, move your ass," I said, tucking my dick back inside my jeans.

I motioned for Dreamer to fill the position I'd vacated, and she immediately pulled off her towel and got to work.

"Dollar-Dollar, wait-oh damn," Honey mumbled, as she gave into Dreamer's tongue skills.

When I turned my attention back on Ashley, she let her towel drop and walked over to her bag by the door. Her body was amazing and she knew it, but I knew I'd break her down like a shotgun if she wasn't careful. I watched as she pulled on a black body suit that hugged every curve perfectly, before she turned back to me expectantly.

"Dreamer, the knife is right there on the bed, you can cut her loose after her third orgasm if you want. We should be back before then," I said, grabbing the key to my Ferrari out of Honey's shorts.

"Dollar!" Honey moaned loudly.

I'd heard that tone many times before, so I knew she was cumming and that made my dick throb with need. I fought it though and led the way outside to the car.

"Where are we going?" Ashley asked, once we were in the car.

"Just to the store, but first, I'm gonna make a call and then we're gonna have a conversation."

I pulled out my phone and quickly dialed the number I needed.

"It's me, I caught up with her."

"You didn't do anything to her, did you?" Aubrey asked.

"Nah, not really, but the situation has changed in a major way. I'll fill you in on that in a little while, but right now I need you to run the following information."

"Give it to me," she replied.

I hold the phone out to Ashley.

"Give her your name, birthday, and social security number."

"Why the hell would you need all that info on me?" she asked distrustfully.

"Because I love that woman you call your sister more than anything or anyone in the world, and if you're not who you say you are or if you ever betray her, I'm gonna kill everyone you ever thought about loving."

I'd made this statement as a matter of fact, but Ashley still looked at me for a few moments to gauge how serious I was. Her putting the phone to her ear and reciting the requested information demonstrated her understanding, and prevented her from meeting her end in the near future.

"Find everything," I said, hanging up the phone and starting the car.

"Had it ever occurred to you that you might get better results if you don't threaten people?" she asked.

I chuckled before pulling off.

"It's probably best that you don't view the things I say to you as a threat, because that implies there's a chance I won't do what I say. I assure you that will never be the case. I'm really not a person who likes to integrate new people into my circle, because I have serious trust issues, but it's obvious that my wife cares about you. So, for that reason I'm willing to let you in, but I need to know who I'm fucking with."

"I guess I can understand that. I want you to know I love Tabitha, and I've always been loyal to her, going all the way back to our days being locked up. I'm here for whatever she needs from me and since you're her dude, I guess that means I'll carry it the same way with you. I ain't with no fuck shit, but I'm with all the bullshit."

Hearing this made me chuckle, because it would seem that my wife only dealt with like-minded people.

"I hear you, just know that I'm always gonna hold you to your word," I replied, pulling up in front of the CVS pharmacy.

I reached in my pocket and pulled out a one-hundred-dollar-bill, passing it to her.

"What do you want me to get?"

"Some condoms," I said, smiling.

"What kind?"

The sudden sexiness that was infused into her voice was clear to see reflected in her green eyes.

"You choose, I trust your judgement."

She flashed me a devilish smile before stepping out of the car. No sooner had she closed the door my phone started vibrating with and incoming text. I quickly scanned Aubrey's preliminary findings on Ashley, liking that nothing jumped out at me as alarming. By the time she made it back to the car I felt comfortable with her being involved for now.

"Here you go," she said, handing me the three-pack of condoms and my one-hundred-dollar-bill. I looked at her with a raised eyebrow.

"No, I didn't steal them, I simply smiled at the cashier," she said, laughing.

It wasn't hard to believe this. I pocketed the condoms, gave her the money back, and pulled off.

"You don't have to give me money, I—"

"I know I don't have to, but I did. I'm not trying to buy you either, but I'ma show you what real is," I said.

Surprisingly, she didn't say anything back and we rode in silence back to the motel room. We walked in to find my wife bent in half and Dreamer with her whole tongue deep in her asshole.

"Well, now, that's interesting," I said laughing.

"Ohhh!" Honey moaned, right before she squirted everywhere.

"That's always a beautiful sight," Ashley said, from beside me.

"Does that mean you've made her squirt before?"

"No, we've never taken it there, but not because I didn't want to," Ashley admitted, smiling.

"So, how would your boyfriend, Jerimiah, feel about you getting dicked down right now?" I asked pointedly.

I knew the surprise on her face was more about my knowledge of her dude than the question of us fucking, but she shook it off quick. Without a word, she took off her clothes and lay down beside Honey on the bed. I followed her lead, stripping down to my socks and taking a condom out of the box. The hunger in Ashley's eyes matched Honey's as they watched me roll the latex slowly down my hard shaft, before I climbed in between Ashley's legs.

"No-no kissing," Honey panted.

"The same goes for you," I said.

With the rules now established, I slowly pushed my way inside Ashley's tight pussy, watching need take ahold of her swiftly. When I was completely inside her, she enveloped me with her long legs, and our battle began. No two pussy's were the same, but we found our rhythm quickly and before I knew it, I was trapped inside the rain of her orgasm. I'd never seen such beauty as watching my wife hold hands with another woman as they both rode the amazing rollercoaster of climax, and it was sexy enough to have me fighting my own fulfillment. When Dreamer repositioned herself so she could sixty-nine with Honey, Ashley moved her legs from around my back to around my neck.

"Fuck-fuck me in the ass," she demanded.

It took me a few moments to work my way inside her, but I pounded her into the waves of her next orgasm within a couple minutes. While she was still speechless, I quickly flipped her over, grabbed her by her hips and dove back inside her pussy, with enough force to make her head bust the headboard.

"Don't k-kill her, bae," Honey said.

"Shut up, Tab!" Ashley said, throwing her ass back fast and hard.

A noisy ten minutes later, we came together, and then it was time to switch. Honey demanded to be cut loose, and then she had me on my back, riding me until she made me say her name while I came inside her. I could tell by the way Dreamer kept touching me as she lay beside me and Ashley ate her pussy that she wanted the dick, but Honey wasn't having it. After Honey came all over my dick, she allowed us to move around again so Ashley could keep sucking Dreamer's pussy, while Dreamer sucked my dick. With Dreamer and Ashley on the bed, and me standing at the foot of the bed, I was able to pick Honey's little ass up and let her wrap herself around my face. She tried to play hard to get, but I wasted no time making her quench my thirst with her delicious cum. I put her back on her feet right before I came mightily down Dreamer's throat. We took a fifteen-minute break, and then we started all over again. Honey and I knew we were in for long days and longer nights away from each other, so we made this moment count. This was the calm before the storm.

Chapter 8
Honey
Three days later

"So, which one of you am I fucking first?" Ashley and I exchanged a look that I knew only we understood, and then she made her move.

"I wanna dance for you first, Ryan, just consider it foreplay," Ashley said, leading him over to his leather recliner, and pushing him down.

"I'm gonna freshen up."

My announcement went completely ignored by Ryan Datton because his eyes were glued to Ashley's seductive body movements. I didn't mind fading into the background, because I needed to have a quick look around Ryan's condo. I knew Kyla wasn't here, but Ryan was the middle child of Eli and Cynthia Datton, so I was hoping to learn something about his mother. Once I talked to Aubrey and told her the man who'd come to my parents' house had said he was working for Eli's wife, she'd dug up all the dirt possible on Cynthia. I was after the information that wasn't in writing though, and I knew her family would know her better than anyone. Eli and Cynthia had three children, and Ryan was lucky number-one on the hit list. I quietly left the living room and made my way down the short hallway to the two bedrooms at the end. I chose the one he obviously used as a work space, and began looking for anything that jumped out at me. Sitting down in front of the laptop on his desk, I pulled my phone from my pocket and dialed a number.

"Bae, I found a computer."

"Okay, turn it on and plug in the flash drive that I gave you," Dollar instructed.

"Hold on."

I put my phone down and did as I was told. I had no idea what the flash drive was doing, but it was obvious by looking at the screen that something was happening.

"Okay, bae, there's a bunch of letters and numbers scrolling across the screen."

"Don't worry, it's doing what it's supposed to do. All you have to do is wait until it stops doing what you see now, unhook the flash drive, and shut it down again before you leave. Be careful, Honey, I love you."

"I love you too," I replied, smiling as I hung up.

I knew the shit we were doing was serious, but I got a giddy pleasure every time I got to work with him. There was an indescribable joy I got from sharing every part of life with the man I believed God had created just for me. It wasn't something I'd ever felt before and it wasn't something I took for granted. The thing I loved about being in this relationship with Dollar was that he didn't encourage my savage side simply for the fuck of it. There was a purpose behind it, and knowing that allowed me to trust him with that part of myself. It wasn't an easy thing to do, especially because I was so used to doing shit my own way, with my own purpose in mind, but that husband of mine made it hard for me not to trust him. Plus, it was better to work side by side, than to keep having to knock me unconscious. That afternoon's little orgy hadn't made the knot on my head any smaller. While the flash drive was doing its thing, I quickly searched Ryan's desk drawers before moving on to his bedroom. The only thing I found was a Taurus .32 pistol in the nightstand, and a safe in his bedroom closet. The safe would have to wait, but I put the .32 in the pocket of my black capri pants before going back to the laptop. With the flash drive secured in my other pocket, I shut the laptop down and made my way back to the living room, in time to see Ashley bending over slowly in front of Ryan.

"You always were flexible," I said, smiling.

"I better be with those long-ass limbs I was blessed with. Are we good?"

"Yeah, let's get down to business," I replied.

"You wanna go in the bedroom now?" Ryan asked eagerly.

"It's time I'm honest with you, Ryan. We didn't pick you up in that bar because we were interested in a threesome, or a night of mediocre sex. I mean, you're attractive for a middle-aged white man, and the fact that you have a nice head of brown hair and straight teeth are positives. My husband's dick is too good for me to go looking for any substitute though," I said.

"It really is though," Ashley agreed, putting her clothes back on.

"I don't, I don't understand," Ryan replied slowly.

I knew that part of his confusion was a result of too many drinks, but I was sure the rest was due to the fact that rich trust fund babies rarely heard the word no. Undoubtedly, it was as foreign to him as the thought of actually accepting it as a final answer.

"Listen to me carefully, Ryan, we're not here to fuck you, we're here to kill you," I said calmly.

The confused look stayed on his face for a few more seconds and then, to my surprise, he grinned.

"I get it now. It's a small community for you working girls, so the others must've told you I like it rough. Don't worry though, I pay extra if I leave any visible bruises," he said.

"Did he just insinuate that we're out here selling pussy?" Ashley asked.

"That was no insinuation, he basically said that shit."

"Oh nah, muthafucka, you—"

"I got this, Ash," I said, pulling out my .22 and screwing on the silencer.

"That's a cute little gun, can I see it?" Ryan asked seriously.

"Sure you can."

I levelled the gun at his right knee, and tapped the trigger before he could move. Naturally, he forgot about rough sex as he cried out in pain, clutching his leg. I grabbed a handful of his hair, yanked his head back, and shoved the still-smoking silencer in his mouth to muffle his screams.

"Shhh, you'll wake the neighbors," I whispered, smiling at the look of terror in his brown eyes.

It took him a few moments of trying to breathe through the pain, before he calmed down enough for me to talk to him.

"Okay, Ryan, now you should know I'm serious about our purpose for being here with you tonight. I'm sure you don't want to die, but there's really no way to prevent that. At this point, the only thing you can control is how much pain you endure before you die. I'm gonna ask you some very simple questions and if you're straight with me, then we won't have an issue, but if you bullshit, I'll cut your dick off a centimeter at a time with a pair of toenail clippers."

"Ouch," Ashley said softly.

"Nod your head if you understand, Ryan, and then I'll take the gun out of your mouth."

He quickly complied and I moved the gun from his throat to his temple.

"Six months ago, your mother sent a man to get my sister's daughter, Kyla, and I wanna know where she is."

"I don't know," he replied swiftly.

I immediately smacked him across his forehead with the butt of the gun, opening up a nice-sized gash that leaked blood like oil from underground.

"Last time I'm gonna ask, before I send my sister here to find your toenail clippers," I warned.

"I-I don't know where Kyla is, she's probably with my mom. My mom doesn't travel without her."

The way he made my stepdaughter sound like a fashion accessory almost got his ass hit again, but I controlled that urge for the moment.

"Where's your mom?" I asked patiently.

"I don't know, she could be anywhere. We have h-homes all around the country and since my dad died, my mom likes to move-move around."

When you came from nothing, you grew up with a distaste for rich people and their brand of bullshit, and the information Ryan was providing was bringing back those old feelings.

"Where's your mom's favorite place to go?" I asked with mounting frustration.

"G-Greece."

"Greece? Like the country?" Ashley asked in disbelief.

This time when I smacked him with the pistol, I hit him in the back of his head, and I did it hard enough to put a dent in his thoughts permanently.

"Don't be a fucking smartass, Ryan. You don't wanna piss me off."

"I'm-I'm telling you the truth, you crazy bitch."

Part of me had known that before I'd smacked him, but it still felt good to do it.

"Last question, Ryan. What's the combination to the safe?"

"Five-seven-five, six-two-eight."

I nodded towards Ashley and she found something to write it down on.

"The safe is in the bedroom closet, check it out," I instructed.

She quickly disappeared, leaving me and Ryan to finish out the business.

"Would you like an open casket or a closed one?"

"Killing me won't get you what you want," he replied.

"Actually, it probably will, but don't you worry yourself over the details. Take comfort in the fact that you didn't die in vain, and you'll have company soon."

"C-company?" he asked, confused.

"Yes, company. I'll tell you a secret. Your mom fucked with the wrong family and now you're all gonna die," I whispered in his ear, laughing softly as I pulled the trigger and blew his brains out.

To my way of thinking he'd gotten off easy, because Dollar would've probably done something medieval to him.

"There was close to a hundred grand in there and this," Ashley said, coming back into the room holding a duffle bag and a chrome, 9mm Berretta.

"Nice. We're done here, so let's go."

After looking around to make sure we weren't leaving anything behind, we made our way to the door. I was in the process of unscrewing the silencer from my pistol, so I could put everything back in my pockets, when a knock at the door froze all movement. The "oh shit" look on Ashley's face was comical, but I motioned for her to chill while I screwed the silencer back on tightly and tiptoed up to the back of the door. When the knocking started again, I signaled for Ash to stash the shit in her hands and answer it.

"Hi, can I help you?" she asked calmly.

"Hi, I'm a friend of Ryan's, is he home?" a female voice asked.

"Sure, come in."

Ashley stepped out of the way and a few seconds later, a chick about my height, with a fucked-up red dye job in her hair stepped through the door. When Ashley closed the door, I raised the pistol and fired two quick shots. Her body hit the floor hard, but by then I was already breaking the gun down and tucking it.

"Alright, now we can go," I said.

We made our way downstairs and outside to the black 2015 Toyota 4Runner Dollar had me drive, since he'd confiscated the Ferrari. Before we pulled off, I called him to tell him we were out of the building, so he could reboot the security system.

"Well, that was easier than I thought it would be," Ashley said, peeling the flesh-colored gloves off her hands.

"Sometimes it's hard, but only when we have to improvise, instead of taking the time out to plan."

"I can tell your husband is meticulous when it comes to planning because he was drilling your ass in preparation for any and everything going wrong," she said, shaking her head.

"I know, but when it comes to taking a muthafucka out, I trust him above nobody else. This ain't simply what he does, it's who he is. Do you think it's weird that it turns me on to know my man is as cold-blooded as they come?"

"Tab, I've known you a long time, and I've heard you talk about your past relationships. Just the way you talk about this man tells me that you're head over heels in love, and there can be nothing weird or wrong about that. Plus, if I'ma keep it all the way real with you, I get it."

"What do you mean you get it?" I asked, making sure to be mindful of the speed limit as I passed a cop.

"When Dollar hit you over the head with that gun, I hopped straight on his ass without hesitation or thought, and he hit me hard enough to make me hop off just as quickly. I didn't need to know who he was because after he put his hands on me, I was prepared to hate him for life. Somehow, finding out he was your husband, the man you'd literally just been raving to me about, and witnessing his love for you despite his knocking you out, changed my opinion. I couldn't believe it or explain it, but I went from wishing I could get ahold of his gun to shoot him with it, to wishing I could suck the skin off his dick!"

"You damn sure tried, bitch," I said, laughing.

"Fuck you! My point is that I get how even the wrong in him feels right, and pulls you in. You better be careful though, because a nicca like that is more powerful and addicting than any drug."

"I wouldn't give a fuck because I ain't never going to rehab!"

We both laughed while high-fiving each other. I would never hype Dollar's head up by telling him that he had me this open, but I was out here literally killing for him, and I felt no guilt. He'd done it for me, and would do it for me without me having to ask. He was my king, I was his queen, and nothing else mattered.

"I've been meaning to ask you though, sis, why did you let me and him fuck? Don't get me wrong, I'm grateful, but I knew how much you hate to share. Not to mention, I saw the way you shut Dreamer down before she could even ask for the dick."

"You damn right I did, I don't know that bitch! What I look like letting my husband fuck some random bitch I know nothing about, because you already know she would've tried to hit him up on the low. I know you and I trust you to keep your long ass legs closed, unless I tell you to open them," I replied, looking over at her to make sure we understood each other.

"I respect that, but I got two questions. Does that mean I can't suck his dick without your permission too? And when are you gonna open your legs for me?"

Her questions made me laugh even though I knew that her crazy ass was serious.

"I'll let you know, okay? Good talk."

"Keep a bitch in suspense then! So, what's our next move?" she asked.

"We wait and see if Ryan's death brings his mom home and in the meantime, we kill all the Dattons we can."

"And what's Dollar gonna be doing while we're doing this?"

"Trust me, he'll be working. The devil don't sleep."

Aryanna

Chapter 9
Dollar
Texas

"Can I help you?"

"Have you heard the good news about our Lord and Savior, Jesus Christ?" I asked, smiling brightly.

"No, and I'm not interested."

I could tell the mildly attractive, slender lady standing in front of me was preparing to close the door on me, but as soon as I opened the Bible in my hand, I saw her expression change.

"Are you sure? Hearing the good news will change your life forever," I said, maintaining my joyful demeanor.

"I-I guess you're right. P-please come in."

She quickly stepped back to allow me to enter her townhouse, but her eyes never looked away from the .25 Smith & Wesson I was holding in between the pages of the good book. God's words were persuasive, but sometimes a little added incentive was necessary.

"Are we alone, Mrs. Norham?" I asked softly, once the door was closed behind me.

"My-my husband is in the kitchen."

"And what about your two daughters, Jeanie and Jennie, where are they, Mrs. Norham?"

"A s-softball game I think."

"Excellent. Please lead the way to the kitchen," I instructed, waving her along with my pistol.

I sat the Bible on a small table that we walked past, because all pretense of me being a solicitor was over, but we would still have a moment of absolute truth.

"H-honey, we have company," Liz Norham announced.

Her husband, Greg, briefly glanced up from the laptop in front of him, before he continued typing whatever he was working on. His bio had said he was a workaholic, but damn, you would think he'd be able to be present in the moment long enough to realize his life was about to end. I calmly removed the silencer from my pocket, screwed it on, and put two bullets into his laptop.

"I see that got your attention, Greg, and since I know you're busy, I won't take up too much of your time. Greg, do you love your wife?"

"Who the hell are you, and why are you in my home with a gun?" he asked, more angry than afraid.

His confusion wasn't believable though, despite the fact that I knew he had a very good idea who I was.

"I'm the man you hired to kill your wife, and that's why I'm in your home with a gun."

The sudden gasp that came from Liz made me look over at her, and the shock on her face indicated she had no idea what her husband had been up to.

"Greg, you piece of shit motherfucker, I—"

"Not so fast, Liz, because I wasn't finished explaining to your husband why I'm here. Greg, I'm also here because I'm the man your wife hired to kill you."

The shock on his face was just as genuine, and now so was the smile on my face.

"I've gotta admit, I've been doing this for a long time, but never have I been in this situation. I mean, Liz, your order came in first, but no sooner had I accepted it I got Greg's email, requesting the same thing. To my way of thinking, there had to have been some type of major event that took place recently that pushed you two to this extreme. I wanna hear about it."

"Are you a fucking marriage counselor, or a goddamn hit man? Shoot that frigid bitch so I can get on with my life!" Greg said angrily.

"My order went in first, asshole, so that means you're the one that's about to die and I'm praying he lets me watch!"

"Oh, I'll do even better than that, if you tell me what happened," I promised.

"The little dick fucker was cheating on me with my own sister, so he deserves to die."

"Her pussy is better than yours, and she loves this little dick! Not every white woman wants to get ran through by some Mandingo warrior, you loose-pussy bitch," Greg replied viciously.

I had been smiling, but hearing what situation had brought this couple to its end had my mind back in the spin cycle that was my own life. One thing I knew for sure was that my wife was way crazier than this bitch, so there was no telling how she would react if she found out I'd fucked Katie. One thing I'd learned from the Norham's is that some secrets had to go to the grave with you.

"Alright, you two are making me sorry I even asked, so just shut up about it. I've come up with an interesting solution of how to solve the problem of who should die though. Liz, does Greg make you cum when you two have sex?"

Her laughter was instantaneous and loud, which immediately had Greg's face red with anger.

"I can tell you're in your feelings, Greg, but that's a good thing. If you can make her cum just by fucking her before she makes you cum, then I'll kill her right here in front of you. Same thing goes for you, Liz."

"W-what? I'm not fucking him, so you can—"

"Bitch, get out of those clothes or die right now," I said, putting the gun to her forehead and cocking the hammer.

Her hesitation was brief, and then she began unbuttoning the white blouse she had on.

"Why are you not getting undressed, Greg? Do I need to shoot you in order to motivate you?"

He quickly shook his head no and began to peel off his blue button-up shirt. Within a few moments, they both were standing there in their underwear, looking at me for further instructions.

"Why do I get the feeling you two fuck in the dark with most of your clothes still on?"

"Because we do," Greg admitted.

"Not today, you don't. Lose the underwear, I want flesh to flesh and you'll be fucking right here on the kitchen floor," I said, backing out of their way.

While they got down to the nitty gritty, I grabbed a can of Coke from the refrigerator, and hopped up on the counter to sit and watch the show.

"Nice body, Liz, it looks like exercise and the real nigga dick of your trainer have both done you good," I commented.

"I knew you were fucking him!" Greg said angrily.

Liz didn't say anything, but she blushed hard enough to turn her whole body red.

"A word of advice, Greg, if you fuck her with all that hatred you feel, you might be surprised by the results. Handle her rough and fuck her like you mean it, instead of like you accidently fell in the pussy."

For a moment, they simply stared at each other and when they actually did start touching, their movements were clumsy and unsure. Suddenly, Greg grabbed her by throat and backed her into a wall before lifting her off her feet, and shoving his dick inside her. I heard the surprise in her moans, but I could see the actual delight all over her face.

"That's right, Greg, fuck her like you missed her," I encouraged, laughing softly.

The sound of a picture falling off the wall and glass shattering were proof of the amount of force Greg was putting into his thrusts, and his wife loved it.

"Th-that's right, fuck me, Greg!" she demanded, grabbing a handful of his hair, while drawing blood from his back with her nails. When Greg spun away from the wall and slammed her down on the kitchen table, the show got interesting enough for me to grab some cookies out of the jar next to me. Live porn was always better than what the internet provided.

"Be careful, Greg, I can hear how wet her pussy is from here."

Instead of heeding my warning, he pulled her to the edge of the table, put her legs on his shoulders and put his pound game to work on her. The sight of Liz's titties bouncing all over the place was arousing, but this wasn't my party, so I was determined to remain a spectator.

"No! No-no-no!" Liz moaned, suddenly trying to scoot away from her husband.

His grip on her was too tight though, because he knew what we all knew. Liz was cumming.

"Oh-oh, God, no!" she screamed, shaking uncontrollably.

A smile of sweet victory lit up Greg's face as he delivered the final strokes that had Liz looking at the back of her eyelids in orgasmic bliss. I brushed the cookie crumbs from my latex-covered fingers and my black suit, before climbing down off the counter and moving over to the kitchen table.

"I told you, didn't I, Greg? Just fuck her like you mean it. The pussy seemed better too, didn't it?"

"Uh-huh."

"I can tell, because you've still got your dick in her. Liz, I know you're kinda torn about the outcome, but before I conclude today's business, do you mind if Greg cums inside you one last time?"

The tears leaking from her eyes had her too choked up to speak, but she managed to nod her permission.

"Thanks for being a good sport about all of this, Liz," I said, putting the gun to her head and pulling the trigger.

I don't know if it was a reflex action that made Greg jump backwards. I just know that he damn near fell.

"Easy, now. I heard about your horses getting spooked, but you've got bad nerves too. It's okay though, go head and get back in the saddle."

"Wh-what?" he asked, confused.

"Liz gave her permission for you to finish and get yours, so go ahead."

"But, she-she's gone. You killed her."

"What's your point?" I asked seriously.

"I'm not-I'm not fucking a dead body."

"It's not like it's cold or anything and dead or alive, she's still your wife. Go ahead and handle your business."

"No, I'm not—"

"Okay, I see what the problem is. You think you have an option, and you don't," I said, calmly putting the gun in his face. When he moved back in between his wife's legs, I repositioned myself so that I was standing behind him.

"You're gonna have to hold her legs for her this time, because she won't be putting them on your shoulders by herself."

It took him a moment to work up the courage to do what he had to do, but when I heard the familiar sounds of Liz's pussy juices back-talking, I knew we were in business.

"See, it feels the same, don't it?"

He didn't bother responding, and he didn't stop fucking her either. Sex for women was eighty-percent physical in my opinion, but for men, it was a one-hundred-percent physical need to release once we were deep off in the pussy. If the sex was bad, most women had to fake it because they couldn't cum, but I didn't know a man alive that wouldn't nut inside something warm and wet. Greg proved my point a few minutes later when his body shuddered from head to toe, and the low moan of fulfillment battled his vocal cords. Before he could move, I jammed my gun to his temple.

"You don't gotta bother thanking me for letting you get that off your chest. It wasn't nothing for a real nigga to do," I said, pulling the trigger.

His body slumped on top of hers in an oddly poetic fashion. I made sure to put his prints on the gun and fire off another shot to make sure he had an adequate amount of gunshot residue on his hand. Once that was done, I set the scene for a murder-suicide, grabbed my can of soda and quietly left the couple to rest in peace. I strolled calmly, but purposefully, to my red Ford F-150 pick-up truck two blocks away, and quickly put the sleepy suburban neighborhood in my rearview. Once I was outside the city limits, I picked up my phone and made a call.

"It's me. I just finished the business, so now I can handle the personal."

"Okay. Emily Datton works in a small book store, and she's at work right now. Do you remember her particulars?" Aubrey asked.

"Seriously? Five foot five, hundred and forty pounds, black hair, green eyes."

"Hey you're the one that taught me the value in being thorough, Dollar, so don't get mad at me."

"Yeah, yeah. Were you able to track down the matriarch of the family?" I asked.

"I was, and she's already been notified about her son's death, so she'll be back in the U.S. anytime now. And when she gets here, she'll get word about two of her cousins dying in a car crash."

"A car crash?" I asked curiously.

"Yeah, according to your wife, it's really dangerous for people to drive under the influence of pills and alcohol."

Hearing this made me chuckle, because it was apparent that my sweet Honey was moving through the Datton family like a force of nature. Not only did I respect that, I loved it because it was sexy as hell, knowing she was more than capable of handling whatever came our way. I'd never known a woman like that, and having her as my own gave me a feeling I could only describe as butterflies. That wasn't gangsta to some niggas, but I prided myself on being different.

"Seems like my baby has a head start, but I'm up to the challenge of catching up," I said.

"Have I told you that you two were made for each other?"

"I couldn't agree more, sis, but to hear you say it still means a lot."

"My only real concern is Katie. Have you decided what you're gonna do about that?"

Her question was one I'd been asking myself since Honey and I had picked her up from prison, but I was still no closer to having an answer than I was then.

"That's tomorrow's problem, right now I gotta do everything possible to get my daughter back."

"Understood, call me when you're done with Emily."

After I hung up, I sent Katie a quick text to see how she was doing. I wasn't as concerned with her physical wellbeing as I was the mental aspect, because she'd taken it incredibly hard when I had to tell her about Kyla. I'd insisted on being the one to do it in anticipation of her reaction though, because I knew when I calmed her down, she'd realize there was no one in the world she could depend on more than me to bring Kyla back. I did unspeakable things for the love of money, so what the fuck did they think I was gonna do for my daughter? It took me twenty minutes to reach the safe house I was using, but with a quick clothing and vehicle change, I was back on the road immediately. Fifteen minutes later, I was pulling up in back of Millennial's used book store. I hopped out of the van and retrieved a box from the back, before making my way to the back door, and pressing the bell for deliveries. A couple minutes later, the door swung outwards and I came face-to-face with Cynthia Datton's youngest child.

"What you got for us today?" she said, smiling.

"Just a box of books that experienced a little water damage. Our local Amazon warehouse got flooded again."

"I would complain or advise your company to invest in a better facility, but that would probably cut our back inventory in half," she replied, laughing.

"Right."

I handed her the box of heavy books and as anticipated, she dropped them. When she bent down to pick them up, I pulled out my .44 revolver and put it to her head.

"If you do anything other than what I tell you easily, you'll die right here and that's a promise. If you cooperate I'll let you walk away when it's over, and that's also a promise."

"We-we don't keep much money in the store, b-but—"

"I'm not here for the money, just get in the van and make sure you climb in through the open driver's side door. I'd hate for you to try and run, because then I'd be forced to shoot you. Now move," I demanded.

She was shaky on her feet, but she still managed to stand up and make it to the van. I got in behind her, and got us on the move.

"Is-is this some type of ransom thing because my-my family has money?" she asked, crying steadily.

"Your family money is of little interest to me, because they took something more valuable that doesn't belong to them."

"Whatever it-it is, I'll make them give it b-back, just please don't hurt me."

"I'm glad you feel that way, because you're my ticket to getting Kyla back," I said, smiling at her.

"Kyla? Why would you…Oh my God, I see it. She's related to you in some way, isn't she?"

"She's my daughter."

My statement didn't stop her tears, but she was now nodding her head in understanding. She thought she understood, but she really had no idea what hell her mother had unleashed on them all. She'd soon learn though. They all would.

Chapter 10
Honey
Texas
Two days later

"Wake up, bitch!" I said, snapping the wet towel in my hand, and popping Ashley's naked ass.

"Ow! Goddammit, Tabitha!"

I laughed while scrambling out of her reach, and winding the towel up again for another assault.

"Bitch, you better not hit me with that towel again, or I'm getting out of this bed and beating your little ass."

"You ain't beating shit, plus you already know you ain't big enough to fuck with me," I replied, looking for the next spot on her body to turn red.

"Tab, why are you fucking with me? You know how tired I am."

"Okay, let's hear it," she replied, reluctantly sitting up and stretching.

It took every ounce of my self-control not to pop her in one of them big ass titties, but I managed.

"Let's kill somebody."

"Haven't we done that?" she asked, confused.

"Yeah, but I mean, I wanna do it like my husband does. I'ma call his sister and take a job to knock someone off for the money."

"I don't know, Tab. I mean, do you think Dollar will let you do that? You remember what happened the last time you went rogue."

"Yeah, bitch, you got some of the best dick of your life, and your skin looks flawless, thanks to him cumming on your face."

"True shit, but I was referring to the part before that, when he smacked life out your ass and hit me with some Mike Tyson shit. I don't think that was fun for either of us, sis, so I'm just asking if you're gonna ask him first."

I knew her concerns were valid, but I was bored as hell waiting on the Datton's to plan their funerals so we could accidentally meet on purpose. When Dollar and I had to wait on the funeral in Chicago, we'd filled the hours with constant rounds of fucking and love making, but my baby wasn't here right now and I missed him.

"I get what you're saying, and yeah I'll ask him, but are you down or nah?"

"I've come this far with your crazy ass, haven't I?" she asked rhetorically.

"Good, now get dressed."

I knew I shouldn't do it but I couldn't resist the urge, and before she knew what had happened, the towel in my hand had popped the hell out of her left nipple.

"Ow! You muthafuckin' bitch!" she yelled, grabbing her boob.

I was laughing so hard I thought I would piss on myself, but the moment I saw the first tear fall from her eyes, I got serious real quick.

"Aw, I didn't mean to hurt you, Ash."

"Fuck you, Tabitha."

I dropped the towel and went to her with open arms, but when she didn't hug me, I knew she was in her feelings for real. I kneeled down in front of her and pried her hand away from her tittie to make sure I hadn't drawn blood.

"You're okay, sweetie, it's just that your nipples are really sensitive."

"No, you play too much, Tab, and I—"

The fact that I now had her nipple in my mouth and was gently sucking on it, changed her words into heavy breathing. It wasn't my intention to start anything, but when she opened her legs, my hand somehow ended up massaging her clit in slow circles. Something about the way she throbbed beneath my touch made my pussy wet, and when I slipped my finger inside her, I found her to be the same way.

"Tab, please-please don't stop," she whispered, arching her back slightly.

My suction increased, causing the softest of moans to escape from between her lips. I bit her gently before switching nipples and repeating my actions. As a woman, I knew there were several degrees of wetness we experienced, and they signaled different things within our bodies. In a matter of moments, Ashley had gone from the wetness of arousal, through the soaking of want, to the tsunami of need. I used one hand to push her down on the bed while removing my other hand from inside her so I could give my tongue a turn. I swam through her pussy lips slowly, drinking from her infinity pool, before moving on to her clit.

"T-Tab-Tab, oh shit!" she moaned.

I sucked on her clit long enough to feel her world ripping apart, and then I sucked her pussy until she begged me to stop. I stood up and looked down at her, admiring the job I'd done of leaving her looking like a fish out of water.

"You good?" I asked, smiling.

Her answer came in the form of laughter, but before I could move she sat up and grabbed me by my hips. We'd known each other for years without taking it to this level, but we'd had enough conversations for her to know what I liked. When her lips immediately locked onto my right nipple and started sucking, right before her teeth grazed it gently, I knew she was trying to make me cum.

"Ash, quit-quit playing," I said weakly.

While her mouth worked one tittie, her hand was seducing the other, and my pussy was only getting wetter. When her mouth switched nipples, she threw my right leg up on the bed next to her left leg, forcing me into a wide stance that allowed her fingers to join the party. I could feel my pussy dripping as soon as she pushed two fingers deep inside me, and the force behind her hand's movement only made me wetter.

"Look at me," she demanded softly.

When I looked down into her sparkling green eyes, I saw a love that had been hidden for a long time, and it shocked me. Before I knew what her intent was, her hand was on my neck, and she was pulling my mouth down to hers. Her kiss was soft, but the song she was playing inside me had increased in both speed and force. Even as her tongue danced with mine, my pussy was squeezing her fingers like they were some good dick, and I could see the end on the back of my eyelids. The feeling of her thumb rubbing steadily on my throbbing clit, while her long fingers dove inside me with a gold medalist's precision finally rocked me, and I came in a wild rush of breathless moans that she swallowed. Suddenly, she grabbed me, spun me, and I found myself on my back on the bed. My legs willingly rested on her shoulders as she used both of her hands to play with my titties, while her mouth performed magic. The feeling of her teeth on my clit forced my back to bend, but her soft hands held me in place.

"Eat-eat this pussy then," I said, wrapping my thighs around her head.

I could feel her whole face trying to crawl inside me, but I didn't worry about her drowning, because the bitch was sucking my pussy like she came with a snorkel. Within minutes, I was squirting down her throat and shaking like two dice in the hands of a hustler.

"Ash, no-no more," I said, when she kept right on eating me.

I told myself I was gonna pull her head away when I grabbed two handfuls of her hair, but the truth was that the head was too damn good for all that. No one except Dollar made me cum back-to-back, but within ten minutes Ashley made me a Laker fan for life, with her ability to show me the meaning of threepeat. When she finally laid down beside me, I didn't know whether to be glad or disappointed, but I was damn sure tired.

"Who knew that cumming took so much energy out of you," I said, yawning.

"I warned you years ago I had that head game that would put your ass to bed."

"True shit, just like I told you I'd make your big ass beg."

We both laughed softly, and somehow our fingers ended up entwined together.

"I love you, Tab."

"Yeah, I know, and I—"

"No, I mean I really love you, bitch. I always have," she confessed.

"You never said anything."

"You know how rare true friendships are, especially under the fucked-up circumstances of doing time, and I didn't wanna ruin ours. Tabitha, you're my ace, and you've been that since day-one. We may fight, argue, disagree, and everything in between, but my love for you never changes."

"At least now when we fight, we can make up properly," I replied laughing.

"So, does that mean you're gonna keep me around?"

Her question made me look at her, and I was surprised to find insecurity masking her beautiful face.

"What type of question is that, Ash?"

"I mean, after all this shit calms down, you're gonna want to get back to your normal life with Dollar and I get that, so I was just wondering where I would fit in."

"Okay, first of all, my life with Dollar will never be normal, not in any sense of the word. You should already know I didn't ask you to walk out on your job and your life just for the purposes of this situation. I love you, bitch, you're my best friend, and really the only one that I feel like I can trust with the secrets of my new life. So, I was kinda hoping you would wanna stick around," I said, squeezing her hand.

I knew the tears in her eyes weren't ones of sadness, because she was smiling at me.

"Does this mean we're not sisters anymore, we're sister wives?"

I had to laugh at the boldness of this bitch, but I knew her question was a serious one.

"That's not something I can answer until we talk to Dollar together, but I'm open to it. I didn't know how I was gonna feel watching him fuck another female, but honestly, seeing him inside you was like him being inside me."

"Aw. I think that's the sweetest thing you ever said to me," she replied, kissing me.

The tender touch of her lips quickly switched to a possessive assault that made my kitty sing with renewed vigor. Before long, our kissing resulted in us tasting and teasing each other simultaneously, until mutual orgasms were reached. We laid together, sweaty and breathless in each other's arms, until sleep was the only thing left to do. When I woke up I felt somewhat satisfied, but there was still an itch I felt needed scratching. I got out the bed, careful not to wake a softly snoring Ashley, and went in search of my cellphone. I called Dollar, but his phone went straight to voicemail, which meant he was either busy or in need of a new phone. It had been a whole day since I'd heard his voice, and I wasn't at all happy about that, because something about being out of touch with him gave me a feeling of being incomplete. He'd warned me that he would be busy with Emily Datton though, so his not answering wasn't exactly a surprise. I still didn't like it though. As far as I was concerned, I'd done what I'd told Ashley I would do, so the next thing I did was send Aubrey a text message, asking if there was any work out here. I expected her to take a while to get back to me, but I didn't get a chance to sit my phone down before it was vibrating with instructions for me to call her. I tiptoed to the bathroom, closed the door, and turned on the shower before dialing Aubrey's number.

"What's up, sis?" I asked.

"You tell me. Are you asking me what I think you are asking me?"

"Yeah."

My response resulted in a heavy silence that I wasn't quite sure how to interpret, but I was smart enough to wait it out.

"Have you talked to Dollar about this?" she asked.

"I tried calling him a couple times, but you know he's busy with that other thing."

"I don't know about this, Honey. I mean, if something were to go wrong you know what Dollar would do to me."

It was on the tip of my tongue to tell her she was being paranoid because Dollar would never hurt her, but the image of him shooting Iree was still vivid in my mind.

"Have I not proven that I can handle myself, Aubrey? Plus, I feel like I need to show my husband that I can handle and fully embrace everything that comes with him. You know like I do that Dollar will never be the type to trust a person off of words, not even me. Only actions matter."

This time, I knew when she got quiet she was chewing on the truth I'd laid out. We both understood the risks of acting without Dollar's knowledge and permission, but I wanted to show my nigga he married his equal in every sense of the word. After a few moments, I heard Aubrey exhale a sigh, and I was hoping that meant she'd do what I wanted.

"Do you know the password to your husband's email?" she asked.

"I do."

"Good, check it in about a half an hour, and get back with me."

She hung up before I could say anything else, but that was okay because I probably would've embarrassed myself by revealing the giddiness I was feeling. It wasn't about killing someone. For me, it was about sharing something else with my soulmate. I put my phone on the sink counter and stepped beneath the hot water's spray. Twenty minutes later, I walked back into the room and over to Ashley.

"Ash, wake up, sweetie," I said, shaking her gently.

She was instantly alert, looking dangerously sexy as she stretched lazily like a big cat.

"How long was I sleep?"

I looked at the phone in my hand.

"It's only a little after four p.m., so it's only been a couple hours."

"Mmm. Are you ready for another round?" she asked, smiling at me.

"Calm down, bitch, this may be the first time you got the pussy, but it won't be the last. Hop in the shower, and I'll let you know what we're doing when you get out."

"Join me," she said, sitting up and grabbing my hand.

I laughed at how insistent she was being, but I was determined to stay focused.

"You don't like to hear the word no, huh? You're starting to remind me of One and a Half Chains."

This made us bust out laughing, because it took us back to our days locked up together. There had been a dyke that looked just like the rapper 2 Chainz and the bitch just would not leave me alone, no matter what I said or did. Ashley wanted to ride that rollercoaster, but I dubbed her One and a Half Chains and told her to have several seats far away from me.

"That's some cold shit to say, Tab, because you know One and a Half Chains was a wild stalker when it came to you."

"My point exactly, she was too thirsty, and you don't gotta be that way. I got you," I replied, giving her a quick kiss while pulling her to her feet.

I smacked her hard on her juicy ass, sending her on her way with a smile. I quickly got dressed, and then logged into Dollar's encrypted email. He'd given me his password to use in case of an emergency, like me having to find him or delete anything incriminating. Technically, this didn't qualify for either situation, but I'd worry about explaining that later. I immediately found the new file folder with my name on it and opened it. Inside were all the details about Tracy Elizabeth Burton, her life, and why she now had to die. The picture that accompanied the file showed an attractive, twenty-eight-year-old, brown-skinned female with a beautiful smile. She wasn't someone you'd look at and think that she was moving kilos of cocaine, but apparently she was and her product had killed the wrong person. I couldn't really judge her because I'd sold dope for most of my life, and there was no doubt in my mind that somebody's child probably overdosed on what I'd been pushin'. That simply meant I could be in Tracy's shoes, but it didn't mean I wouldn't take that bitch out of her shoes. I carefully read through all the info Aubrey had provided, using the tactics Dollar had taught me when it came to looking for the weaknesses to exploit in order to make the job as easy as possible. I knew that normally, Dollar would request a car and weapons, but we had a car and enough clean guns to handle this. I sent an email to Aubrey telling her that, and then I got to work planning.

"You look entirely too serious and tense for a woman who's had multiple orgasms today," Ashley said, coming back into the room, drying off.

"Get dressed, we gotta go to Louisville real quick."

"Louisville? What for?"

I just looked at her for a second, and then I smiled.

"Seriously? Dollar actually went for it?" she asked, somewhat surprised.

"I got the info on the bitch we're about to go see right here on my phone, so get dressed."

While she did that, I gathered everything we needed, and loaded it in the 4Runner. Ten minutes later, we were on the move, embracing the darkness falling all around us. I told Ashley all about Tracy on the drive to her house, but I still didn't have a solid plan.

"Wow, this is way too nice to be a trap house," Ashley said, looking at Tracy's townhouse.

"She don't sell dope here, this is where her and her daughter stay."

"Alright, you got us here, Tab, now what?"

I was just about to confess that I didn't know when a cotton candy pink, old school Monte Carlo pulled up across the street in front of Tracy's car, but I was surprised at the opportunity that had just presented itself.

"Pass me the 9mm," I said, slipping my gloves on quickly.

I took the gun from Ashley's outstretched hand, checked it, flipped off the safety, and stepped out of the truck. I scanned my surroundings, but I spotted no one on either side of the dark street. As soon as Tracy got out and closed the car door, I raised the gun, and started dumping bullets at her. I was used to firing with a silencer on a gun, so the roar of the cannon in my hand was startling, but I didn't let up. Two of my first four shots hit their mark, throwing Tracy on the hood of her car. I advanced on her quickly, put the gun to the back of her head, and permanently turned off her satellite with a final shot. I turned to go back to the 4Runner, but I was suddenly frozen by the sight of Tracy's fifteen-year-old laying on the ground on the other side of the car. I could see the single bullet hole in her chest leaking blood, and her eyes were shut, but she was still breathing. The question was, did I finish her or run?

Aryanna

Chapter 11
Dollar
Tennessee

"Wow, you look like shit."

"Thanks," I replied sarcastically, stepping aside so Rose could enter the house.

"I didn't expect to hear from you so soon, but from the looks of things, you ain't slept since you finished up your business in Florida."

"It feels like that, but I've only been up two days. I think," I said, rubbing my eyes and looking at my watch.

The concept of time didn't really make much sense right now, because my brain was moving off of reflex and instinct. I'd been moving non-stop since abducting Emily in Texas, and I was now too scared to stop, for fear my body would shut itself down for the next four days. I didn't have time to waste like that. I wanted my daughter in my arms as soon as possible. Rose had proven herself reliable when I'd had to bring my reign of terror to Florida, and I trusted she would do the same now.

"I know you called me out here to work, but if you've been up for two days, Dollar, I'm gonna need you to sleep first."

"Believe me I want to, but this situation is too serious to waste a moment. It involves my daughter."

"Tell me what happened," she said, sitting beside me.

I ran the important shit down to her, leaving out the triangle of Honey, Katie and me, because Kyla was the focus.

"So, what do you need me to do?"

In response to her question, I got up and grabbed a small red cooler I'd had sitting by the door.

"I want you to deliver this for me, along with a cellphone I'ma give you. There's a video on the phone."

"What's in the cooler?" she asked, taking it from me.

"A tongue, a nipple, a finger, and a toe."

She stared at me for a moment, trying to see if I was serious.

"Where's the best of the body?" she asked.

"Downstairs in the basement, resting in a custom-made dog cage. She's alive though, but currently sleeping off the anesthesia from her surgery."

"Surgery."

The way she said that one word while squinting at me made me chuckle.

"Well, after I removed a few souvenirs, I had something added to her, but it was professionally done by a doctor who's paid not to ask questions."

"The doctor may not ask questions, but I damn sure have a few. I've seen firsthand how crazy you are, Dollar, so what did you do, sew a dick onto this bitch's forehead?"

The imagery of that question made me laugh out loud.

"Nah, I ain't do no shit like that, but if I had a spare dick laying around, I might have tried it. All I did was put a half a block of C-4 in her pussy, and then had her pussy sewed shut."

For a moment, I could tell she was waiting on the punch line to that joke or for me to start laughing, but when I did neither, she simply shook her head.

"So, what you're telling me is that you literally made a bitch's pussy dynamite?"

I laughed again, nodding my head in approval for the way she phrased that.

"Yeah, I did that, and when the time comes, I'ma exchange her for my daughter."

"And blow up the chick, along with whoever she's around," Rose said, nodding in understanding.

"Exactly. First I need you to deliver the cooler and this phone to this address."

I pulled the phone and a slip of paper from the pocket of my jeans, and passed them both to her.

"You got the key to this house we're in?"

"Yeah, why?" I replied, confused by her question.

"Because, while I'm gone I want you to sleep, and I'll wake you up when I get back."

"You know that you're not old enough to try and make me do something, right?" I asked.

"Age ain't got shit to do with it, neither does the fact that you and I ain't fucking, in case that crossed your mind as an excuse not to listen. You know I'm right about you needing sleep, just like I've been right about other things in the past, so arguing is really pointless. Key please."

The serious expression on her face and the way she held out her hand expectantly said that not only was the argument over, but I'd lost.

"I'm starting to like you more and more, Rose. Maybe one day, we will fuck."

"I'll let you know if I want some dick, but business comes first."

Her quiet confidence was sexy, but she was right about focusing on the business at hand. I dug the house key out of my pocket and gave it to her.

"I'll show myself out, you just lay down."

"Yes, ma'am," I replied, doing just that once she got up off the couch.

Once she closed and locked the door behind her, I closed my eyes, but I quickly snapped them open when I realized I finally had a free moment to call Honey. I was known to have a one-track mind when I was handling business, but my beautiful wife had crossed my mind more times than I could count since we last spoke. It felt strange to miss somebody as much as I did her, but I was okay with it. I'd learned that when it came to Honey, it was pointless trying to control my feelings, because I was all the way fucked up about her and happy about it. I pulled my phone out and turned it on, not surprised to find a dozen missed calls from Honey. Having the same amount of missed calls from Aubrey disturbed me a little though, making me call her back first.

"It's me, what's up?"

"Have you-have you talked to Honey?" she asked hesitantly.

"No why?"

"Call her."

It was on the tip of my tongue to shoot rapid fire questions at Aubrey's head, but she'd already hung up. Part of me wanted to call her ass back, but I was already dialing Honey's number swiftly.

"D-Dollar?" she answered immediately.

Right away I could tell that either she'd been crying or she still was crying, and my heart hit my feet.

"What's wrong? Are you hurt? What happened?"

"I'm-I'm not hurt, but I-I fucked up, bae. I fucked up bad."

"Okay, just calm down and tell me what happened," I encouraged.

"I can't, not on the phone."

That one statement made my heart beat faster in my chest, but I kept my voice smooth as silk.

"Okay, baby, where are you and Ash right now?"

"In the motel room in Kentucky."

"I want you to give Ashley the phone real quick."

There was a brief rustling sound and then Ashley was on the phone.

"I'm here, Dollar."

"Is she okay, Ashley?"

"Physically, yeah."

Hearing that didn't make me feel any better, especially because I wasn't right by her side.

"I'm in Knoxville, are you familiar with the city?" I asked.

"Yeah, I know it."

"Get in the truck and don't stop until you get here. I'm texting the address to Honey's phone right now."

"We're on the way," she replied, hanging up.

I quickly sent my location with instructions not to stop for nothing or no one, and then I called Aubrey back.

"What the fuck happened?" I growled through clenched teeth.

"Did you talk to your wife?"

"Yeah, I talked to her, and she told me she can't talk about it over the phone. I'm expecting you to be able to tell me what the fuck this is all about, Aubrey, so spit it the fuck out because you're trying my patience."

"She took a job."

Those four words said so much, while leaving me with more questions than I wanted to beat Aubrey over the head with. Honey had been right to say it couldn't be discussed over the phone, but from where I was sitting that was the only thing she'd done right. She had no business fucking around with my business without me or my permission, and she was smart enough to know that. So was Aubrey.

"What part of your brain thought that was a good idea?" I asked with an icy calm.

"She-she said that—"

"Shut up, Aubrey, because you know better. You just better be glad nothing physically happened to her."

I hung up before she could try to get any more lame shit out of her mouth. I could feel my heartbeat pounding in my temples, forcing me to take slow deep breaths to calm myself down. I loved Aubrey, but if she'd been standing in front of me, I would've examined her brain personally. I knew she understood Honey was different in the sense that she was capable of dealing with my lifestyle, and even participating when necessary, but Honey wasn't a person who killed for the fun of it. A killing for her had to make more sense than just dollars, and I understood that. I was hoping that Honey's fuck-up hadn't been anything more than her freezing up, or maybe exchanging shots with whoever she'd made a move on. In my mind, the fact she wasn't physically hurt meant that whatever happened could be dealt with easily. For me, the biggest problem right now was having to wait. Sleeping would've been nice, but the mere idea of that was forgotten. I spent a nerve racking three hours pacing throughout the house, constantly checking the Kentucky news on my phone, until I spotted the black 4Runner pulling up. I opened the front door and barely had time to brace myself before Honey launched all five foot four, hundred and fifty pounds of herself at me.

"I got you, baby," I said, rubbing her back as I carried her to the couch.

The sound of her sobbing tore at my heart, making me clutch her trembling body closer to mine.

"Shhh, it's okay, baby. Whatever it is, we can fix it," I said softly.

She looked at me with so much sadness in her eyes and shook her head, before burying her face back in my chest, and crying harder. I sat with her in my lap and simply held her while she got it out, but the longer she cried, the more worried I got. When I looked to Ashley for answers, she made the motion of shooting at someone, which explained absolutely nothing.

"Honey, you need to tell me what happened, so I can make our next move."

It still took her a few minutes to pull herself together, but eventually the shaking subsided and the sobs stopped.

"I-I took a job. We went to-to scout her house and while we were there, the target pulled up. I j-jumped out and started shooting. I k-killed her."

Despite the fact that she'd stopped talking, I somehow knew that wasn't the end of the story.

"Did anyone see you?" I asked.

"I don't t-think so."

"Okay, well then, what aren't you telling me, baby?" I asked confused.

She opened her mouth to speak again, but all that came out was strangled cry, followed by more tears.

"Ashley, what am I missing?"

"The chick had her fifteen-year-old daughter in the car with her, but because it was dark, Tab didn't see her. She took a bullet to the chest and died," she replied softly.

I understood immediately why Honey was distraught. Even though she was a beautiful savage, there were still some things she wouldn't do. She might not judge me for all the shit I did, but at the end of the day she still had a soul, which meant that she had a conscience. Right now it was that very thing that was weighing her down in the pool of her own tears, and I didn't know what to say to ease what ached. I could've criticized her decision to insert herself into something that she didn't fully understand, but I knew she'd learned a lesson that my words wouldn't do justice. Her statement to me on the phone about her fucking-up made perfect sense now.

"Sweetheart, you didn't mean to kill that girl, and anyone who knows you knows that. I understand that knowledge doesn't undo what you did, but you have to understand that nothing can be done to turn back the hands of time. As harsh as it sounds, this is one regret you're gonna have to learn to live with."

"It's too h-hard, bae, she was j-just a k-kid. She was Rain's a-age. That could've b-been my daughter," she replied, crying harder.

I should've known she would put herself in the shoes of this particular target, given the age similarity to Rain. I'd been content to let her cry, but she was getting borderline hysterical.

"Where's the bathroom?" she suddenly asked, panicked.

"Down the hall, first door on the right."

She hopped out of my lap and ran in that direction, and a few seconds later I knew why. The sound of violent vomiting echoed back into the living room, like Honey was equipped with surround sound.

"Has she been like that the whole time?" I asked.

"Pretty much. I had to pull her off the street and into the truck because after she dome checked the bitch, she simply stood there and watched the little girl bleed out."

"What the fuck made you two do some crazy shit like that anyway, Ashley?"

"Wait, you mean you didn't know we were doing a job?"

The look I levelled at her said it all.

"Dollar, I swear to you I told her to call you first, and I naturally assumed that you'd approved when she had all the info on the bitch. If I had known, I wouldn't have let her do it."

I really wanted to be pissed at Ashley, but what she'd said made too much sense, and we both knew that my wife was a renegade. The question was what did I do now? When I caught sight of her walking slowly back up the hallway, eyes puffy and still leaking tears, I knew I had to do the merciful thing. I quickly pulled the Glock 9mm from the small of my back, ejected the clip, and ejected the bullet in the chamber before Honey realized what I was doing.

"Seriously, Dollar?" Ashley whispered.

I silenced her protest with a single look.

"You feel better, bae?" I asked, sincerely.

"N-no."

"Come here, come to daddy," I said sweetly.

She moved towards me without hesitation, and when she got within arms' reach I grabbed her, spun her, and smacked her over the head with the pistol. Unlike last time though, I actually caught her before she hit the ground, and laid her on the couch.

"You're gonna give her brain damage if you keep that shit up," Ashley said, in a disapproving tone.

"No, what I'm gonna give her is the rest she needs because she's mentally exhausted, and emotionally overwhelmed. I've got something here to help her sleep, but you know she wouldn't have taken it willingly."

"True. So, what's your plan?" she asked.

"I'ma dope her up and you're gonna take her home to Mississippi. I should have everything wrapped up here shortly, and then I'll be down there."

"What do I tell her when she wakes up?"

"Tell her I love her, no matter what."

Aryanna

Chapter 12
Honey
Mississippi
Two days later

I could feel the pounding in my brain as soon as I woke up, and it was fierce enough to force me to keep my eyes shut. The warmth of sunlight was heating my eyelids, making me silently pray that God would turn off the sun just for a little while. I knew damn well that I hadn't gotten blackout drunk, but I felt like the worse hangover ever was only a deep breath away. Was I high? I couldn't remember scoring any dope, even though I remember desperately wanting some to numb the pain I felt, and erase the memory of what I'd done. Seeing as how I hadn't forgotten shit, I probably wasn't amongst the clouds. So, why did it sound like Iree was yelling somewhere close by? I could barely make out the sounds of a heated argument, but the voices involved sounded familiar. Against my better judgement, I opened my eyes and found a familiar sight that made no sense. I'd known the bed I was laying in was too comfortable to be the same one from the motel, but I didn't realize that was because it was my own bed. Somehow, I was at home in Mississippi, in the bedroom I shared with my husband. Did that mean what I remembered about killing a fifteen-year-old girl had been nothing more than a horrible nightmare? I sat up in the bed, preparing to go find out, but my stomach rolled hard enough to let me know what direction I was headed first. I bolted for the bathroom and managed to baseball slide to a stop in front of the toilet, just in time to blow chunks in the water. It felt like I spent an eternity hugging the toilet bowl, but I eventually made it on my feet and over to the sink. The reflection in the mirror said hot-ass mess. My eyes were almost swollen shut, my hair was in danger of becoming a bird's nest, and the bags under my eyes were heavy enough to be filled with gold bricks. Throwing up had made me feel a little better though, even with the yelling I could still hear in the distance adding to my headache. While I had the strength, I stood at the sink and got myself together until I felt somewhat normal. By the time I'd made it back into the bedroom, the argument I'd heard had gotten louder and now I was positive that was Iree's voice, along with Katie's. I grabbed the .45 that we kept under the mattress, and followed the loud screaming outside to the front porch. Iree and Katie were standing toe to toe, and Ashley had a hand on each woman's chest to keep them apart. I quickly flipped the safety off, raised the pistol, and fired two shots over their heads.

"Both of you bitches shut up before I give you something to holler about," I said angrily.

"You better get your sister, Honey, before I kill her," Iree warned.

"Little girl, you ain't killing shit except my goddamn patience," Katie replied.

I could tell they were about to start their bullshit again, but the sight of me pointing the gun at one and then the other silenced them.

"Iree, I don't know where Rain is, but go find her and spend some time with her. Smoke a blunt, take a walk, I don't care, just go," I demanded.

I thought she was gonna punch Katie in the face first, but thankfully she just turned and stormed off inside the house.

"You're too goddamn old to be fighting with kids, Katie," I said.

"She started it."

Her response left me tempted to shoot her ass again, but I knew that it damn sure wouldn't be in the leg this time.

"Ashley, what…"

I let my sentence trail off as my brain processed what Ashley being here actually meant. The gun in my hand suddenly matched the weight of my heavy heart, forcing me to lower it as I fought the urge to cry. I may not have remembered how I got home, but I damn sure remembered the endless crying I'd done.

"Katie, if you're gonna stay here, then you're gonna have to learn how to get along with Iree. She's as much Dollar's daughter as Kyla, and I'd advise you to keep that in mind because at the very least you want a good co-parenting relationship with Dollar. I don't care who started today's bullshit, you're thirty-two and she's sixteen, which means you're twice her age. Act like it please. I love you, so don't make me choose between you and my husband, because that ain't fair."

"That's not what I'm trying to do, sis, and I've done my best to stay out of that little bitch's way, but for some reason she just doesn't like me."

"This house is big enough for you two to avoid each other, but if you think it would be easier for you to go to a hotel just say the word, and we'll cover the cost," I offered.

"No, I wanna be here with you and Dollar. I think shit will be easier with you and him back here."

"Wait, Dollar's here?" I asked, confused.

"No, but—"

The sound of a vehicle approaching halted Katie's words, and a few seconds later I saw the black 4Runner I'd been driving come into view moving up the driveway. It wasn't until then that I noticed the Ferrari already parked next to my parents' car.

"Ashley, did you drive us here in Dollar's Ferrari?"

"Yeah, he told me to and he kept the truck."

"And how long ago was that?" I asked.

The way Ashley's face turned a bright red indicated that it hadn't been hours, but based on the vague memory I had of the last time I was around my husband, I thought I knew what happened.

"He knocked me out again, didn't he?"

"Yeah, but you needed to rest. That's the only reason he did it," Ashley replied.

I calmly removed the clip and the bullet in the chamber from the pistol in my hand, and put them in my pocket. Then I hid the gun in my hand behind my back.

"That's not a good idea, Tab," Ashley warned.

"I know."

"Let me get my daughter before you do some dumb shit," Katie said, heading down the porch steps towards the truck.

"He got Kyla back?" I asked, surprised.

"Yeah, he called and told us a little while ago that he was bringing her home," Ashley replied.

Hearing this made me smile for the first time in a long time, but just as quickly, my anger was back.

"Exactly, how long was I unconscious, Ash? And if you lie to me, I'll shoot you."

"It's been two days."

I knew Dollar probably had reasons he felt were extremely valid to knock me out, and give me instructions to keep me sedated, but that didn't make me any less angry. I maintained my composure though, and kept a neutral expression on my face as Dollar got out and reunited my niece with her mother. When our eyes locked, I could tell he was trying to check my temperature, so I smiled at him like he was my hero and waited patiently for him to make his way over to me.

"I've missed you so much, baby, you just don't know," he said, coming up the stairs.

"I missed you too, bae, so get your ass over here already."

My smile stayed in place until he was close enough for me to strike, and then I let the devil out. The element of surprise worked to my advantage, allowing me to catch him flush on the side of his head with the butt of the gun, but I wasn't packing enough power to drop him. I cocked my arm back to swing again, but suddenly the gun was knocked from my grasp and I was lifted off my feet.

"Put me down, goddammit!" I yelled, struggling against his powerful grip.

"Calm your little ass down," he growled, carrying me around the side of the house.

"Fuck you! You hit me with your pistol for the last time, nigga! Now you see how that shit feels!"

I was still struggling to get loose, but the way he'd thrown me over his shoulder made it impossible. It crossed my mind that I might've gone too far to turn back seeing as how there'd been blood running from his scalp instantly. I wouldn't show him fear though, and I wouldn't cower before him. I'd done that with relationships in the past and it only made matters worse, not better. I was probably about to get the shit beat out of me at the least, but I was going down kicking and screaming. When we got to the back corner of the house I suddenly found myself on my feet with my back up against the house and Dollar towering over me. I imagined the look in his eyes at this exact moment was the last thing that people saw before they ran into the fork in the road between heaven and hell. It made my soul shiver, but I was still determined not to show fear. Fear to any animal was an invitation to get eaten, and Dollar wasn't a normal creature. He was at the top of all food chains. I kept waiting for him to say or do something, but he just kept staring as his blood dripped steadily down the side of his face and onto his clothes.

"If you're gonna kill me, then—"

I never got to finish my thought before he launched an unexpected attack. The feeling of his lips on mine startled me, but I was able to recover swiftly and our kisses became a heated battle that made my body temperature rise. I felt the button on my jeans pop off as he grabbed at them, pushing them and my panties to my feet. I kicked one leg free while simultaneously unzipping his jeans and pulling his hard throbbing dick out. It was exactly two seconds later, when my feet once again left the ground, and I found myself pinned to the house by his violent invasion inside me.

"Dameian!" I choked out, holding onto him tightly.

Each stroke felt like his dick was at war with my uterus, and he was literally beating down all doors to get to it. I could feel the wetness of my pussy go from zero to a hundred, but I remained tight enough to have him breathing hard already. To keep from screaming out, my lips found his neck and I bit down with a pit bull's determination. This only seemed to motivate him though, because the pounding he was delivering increased in both power and speed. I could feel his blood dripping steadily onto my face and I could taste it, mixed with what was already on my tongue from me biting him, but I didn't care. We'd become the definition of giving each other life.

"I-I love you, Dameian!"

"Fuck you!" he growled, drilling me harder still.

134

Moments later, I came hard enough to put tears in my eyes, and I felt him quickly follow me out of this world into the universe of cosmic orgasms. For a while he stood there, holding me up against the wall with his dick still pulsating inside me, staring at me in a way that touched every fiber of my being. He leaned in to kiss me again, gently this time, before pulling out of me and putting me down. He quickly took his shirt off and wiped the blood off of my face before doing the same to himself, and wiping the blood from his head. I put his dick back in his jeans and hurriedly put my clothes back on before someone caught us. The fact that he'd been so bold as to fuck me right here in broad daylight, with all the people we had roaming around out here having the ability to catch us, turned me on enough to have my pussy still tingling. Somehow, I knew it wasn't the time to press my luck by going another round.

"I'm sorry I hit you," he said sincerely.

"I know why you did it I just didn't give myself a chance to accept it. I didn't wanna think about or feel the guilt that almost swallowed me because of-because of—"

"We don't have to talk about that ever again. If you need to though, I'm here and I understand," he said.

The unconditional love that I felt for him in this moment put tears back in my eyes, but I wasn't about to cry when there was actually something to celebrate.

"How did you get Kyla back so quickly?"

"I sent pieces of Emily Datton to her mom with a video of how they were removed, and I made it clear that I was only gonna keep chopping her up until she fit nicely into my crock pot. Once Cynthia figured out there was no way around meeting my demand, she agreed to the exchange."

"You know you're gonna have to move on her before she makes a move against us, right?" I asked.

The smile he turned on me gave me chills, but I simply shook my head and grabbed him by the hand. I led him back around to the front of the house, past a curious looking Ashley sitting on the stairs, and inside to the room Denise and Savannah had claimed as theirs.

"See if he needs stiches," I said, leaving him in their capable hands.

While that was taken care of, I went back outside and retrieved my pistol off the porch.

"Your ass is fucking crazy," Ashley said, shaking her head.

"Yeah, I know, but he brings it out in me sometimes."

"Was it worth it, and before you ask me what I mean, you should already know that I followed you two to make sure he didn't kill your dumb ass." I laughed softly while watching Katie play with Kyla in the grass a few yards away.

"I won't lie to you, Ash, there aren't words for what happens between us in those moments of high emotion. There's a twisted beauty in what he and I become, and I love it, but it scared me too, because I know the line we walk is thin and neither of us is in control. In those moments he could kill me and I wouldn't care, because I love him that much. I know he feels the same way."

"Wow," she whispered.

I didn't hear judgement in her voice, but I wouldn't have given a fuck if she did judge me. She'd never grasp all that Dollar and I shared. No one would or could, because our connection was on a totally different level than any relationship one could compare it to. We were one, it was that simple or that complicated, depending on how you looked at it.

"You sure you wanna stick around? Shit tends to get crazy," I asked, looking over at Ashley.

"I see that, but the love is real. I wanna be a part of that."

"Always remember I gave you the opportunity to leave, because now your ass is stuck with us," I said smiling.

"Bitch, I already knew that, I'm just hoping Dollar sticks me like he did you because-mmph!"

The expression on her face made me laugh, but it also reminded me of some pressing business needed handling.

"Do you still have the key to the Ferrari?" I asked.

"Yeah, it's right here in my pocket."

"Okay, I want you to run to the store for me. Hold on while I go get you some money."

"I don't need money, just tell me what you need," she said, standing up and stretching.

I looked around to make sure nobody was within hearing range before I spoke.

"A pregnancy test."

"What?" she exclaimed loudly.

"Shhh, bitch, don't cause no fucking scene, because I don't know for sure yet! Just go get it for me."

"I got you," she replied, grinning as she put a hand on my stomach before leaving.

"Where's Ash going?" Dollar asked, coming outside.

"To the store, but she'll be right back."

"Oh, okay, well we have another problem. This house is too damn crowded, bae! I'm surprised that nobody caught us a little while ago," he said.

"That didn't stop you from fucking the shit out of me, though. I hear what you're saying because right now, I'd love for you to pull your dick out and fuck my face right here."

The look he gave me signaled an internal struggle that made me laugh out loud, because I knew I'd made his dick hard just by putting the idea in his head. I had no doubt he'd make me pay for it later, and I was looking forward to it.

"That was cruel, bae, but it proves my point. I've got a plan though. After Thanksgiving, we'll take your parents and the kids home, and then we're gonna get Savannah and Denise a condo in town. That'll make it easier for them to establish a routine if they want to volunteer or work at the local hospital. Plus, now that you've got Ashley, you don't need them around to satisfy your carnal pleasures."

"Speaking of Ash, she wants to be my sister-wife."

I could tell what I'd said caught him flat-footed, and the expression on his face was once again comical enough to make me laugh.

"How do you feel about that?" he asked cautiously.

"I'm good with it I think. I love her, and I trust her around what we do. I also don't wanna shoot her in the face at the thought of you fucking her, so that's a plus. It don't hurt that the pussy is good too."

I was wondering why my last statement caused him to look at me with raised eyebrows, until I remembered that I wasn't supposed to know her pussy was good.

"Don't judge me, Dollar, just love me."

"Whatever you say, baby. It sounds like we're about to be one big dysfunctional family."

"Does that include us?' Katie asked from behind me.

I turned around to find her standing at the bottom of the stairs, holding a sleeping Kyla in her arms.

"Of course it does, sweetie, you know we wouldn't turn you and Kyla away," I replied.

"Good, because I want her to know her aunt Tab. I want her to know her daddy too."

I watched Katie's eyes skate past me to Dollar, and the fact that she smiled kinda threw me off. They must've had a hell of a conversation while I was gone.

"Thank you, Katie," Dollar said.

"Like I told you, Kyla was created in love, so it's only right that she know that."

I tried not to give an outward reaction to hearing Katie talk about the love she used to share with my husband, but inside, the savage was warning that bitch to chill.

"I need to take care of something before we get settled in though," Katie said.

"What's that?" I asked.

"I need to go to Florida for a few days and see Dad."

Aryanna

Chapter 13
Dollar
Mississippi
Two weeks later

"When do you sleep?" Katie asked, coming to stand beside me at the door to Kyla's room.

I'd heard her approaching, and even though I'd been somewhat avoiding her, the sight of my sleeping daughter was too beautiful to walk away from.

"She's amazing. I can sleep anytime, but I missed so many moments like this, that there's nowhere else I'd rather be."

"I know the feeling. I lose track of how many times I get up every night to check on her," she confessed.

The room Katie was staying in was big enough for her and Kyla to live in, but it had been important for both of us to give our daughter her own room, and fill it with toys. Katie and I came from the mud, but Kyla would never have that same dirt under her nails. On this Katie and I agreed, even though she was constantly cautioning me against spoiling our daughter. I wasn't trying to hear none of that shit though, I was in love in a way I'd never been before. I'd fallen deeper every day I'd gotten to spend with Kyla over the last two weeks. At first, I'd worried that feeling the way I did would somehow make me weak or soft, but I felt even more ferocious, because I knew what I'd do to protect my daughter. What I'd done to Emily Datton wasn't even the tip of the iceberg.

"Is it weird that we stand here watching her like this?" I asked.

"Since when do you give a damn what's weird?"

We both laughed softly at the truth.

"You know what I mean, Katie. I've more or less raised Iree, but this is still unchartered territory for me."

"You're doing great, and Kyla loves you already. Speaking of your other daughter though, can you please tell me what the fuck her problem is with me?"

I'd managed to keep Iree and Katie from physically clashing over the past week, since Honey and my in-laws had left for Alabama, but it hadn't been easy. Even though the looks Iree delivered weren't directed at me, I could still feel their heat, and I knew her dislike for Katie was real.

"Iree is a loyal person, and her loyalty lies with Honey."

"Okay, but that's my sister, so why would Iree feel like she has to choose sides?"

"Because she knows what happened between us that night," I replied, looking at her with a knowing look.

"Oh."

I could tell she understood, but there wasn't an ounce of regret on her face. My feelings about our indiscretion changed daily, but a lot of that had to do with my feelings about Katie's father. True enough, he deserved to die, but now I had to figure out how that would affect Katie, and by extension, my daughter. Honey and I had thus far been able to discourage Katie from going to Florida until she actually talked to her dad, and I did my best to distract her from the idea by continuing to rebuild my friendship with her. That kinda made it impossible not to think about the night we shared together. Sometimes, when she looked at me, I knew she was thinking about it, and I worried that anyone around us would know or somehow smell the old sex on us. I knew it was dangerous to keep Katie close, but the alternative was worse for different reasons. My eyes swung around to my sleeping angel, knowing that I couldn't do anything to jeopardize her position in my life. I loved her too much to lose her.

"Did you tell her that it was a one-time thing that won't happen again?"

"We didn't actually talk about it because that's when all hell broke loose and I had to leave. She won't say shit though, if that's what you're worried about," I replied confidently.

"Okay, but don't you think Tab is gonna start to question why Iree is so openly hostile towards someone she barely knows? You know my sister ain't stupid, and if it wasn't for all the craziness that's been going on with the holidays, she would've picked up on it already."

"I know. I'll speak to Iree," I said.

"Maybe-maybe it just wasn't a good idea for all of us to live here."

Hearing this made my head quickly snap back around to her, but I paused before speaking, so that I could choose my words carefully.

"Are you suggesting that Iree move out, or that you do?" I asked, making it clear that under no circumstance was Kyla going anywhere.

"Dollar, I would never ask you to choose between us, but you know it's not good for Kyla to grow up around constant hostility, especially directed at her mother. I'm just saying that maybe it's a good idea to put some space between us for a little while."

"And how do you suggest we achieve that, Katie?"

"You said you would speak to her, and I trust you to do that. I'm hoping by the time Kyla and I get back from Florida, you've convinced her to be civil at the least."

"Florida? Have you spoken to your father?" I asked, knowing that was impossible.

I knew where his head was buried though, if she really wanted some face time.

"No, not yet, but his wife is due back from some extend-ed business trip she's been on, so I'm gonna contact her before we go."

"You're not going to Florida," I said calmly.

"Excuse me?"

Her tone of voice suggested we were about to clash like the titans, but I would be damned if we did it here. I took her by the hand and led her down the stairs, and outside into the moonlight.

"Get in," I demanded, stopping at my Ferrari.

Even in the darkness, I could see the attitude etched in the lines of her face, but she climbed into the passenger's seat. Once I was behind the wheel I took a few moments to let her calm down, and I used the time to figure out what approach I wanted to take. Somehow, I knew telling her that her dad was dead wasn't what I should lead with.

"You wanna go for a ride?" I asked.

She didn't answer at first, but when she looked at me, I didn't feel as much heat coming from her.

"Might as well, since we're already in the car."

I dug the key out of my pocket, started the car, and eased away from the house. Once I reached the end of the drive-way and turned onto the main road, I stood on the gas, and let the car scream into the night.

"Don't kill us, Dollar."

"Relax, I got this," I replied, shifting gears with the flick of my finger.

Despite having a good rapport with local law enforce-ment, I still didn't press my luck by running this street beast through town, instead electing to stay on the back roads and stick to the outskirts. Ten minutes later, I brought us to a stop on a dead-end road, and shut the car off.

"Are you gonna explain why you're determined to keep me out of Florida, Dameian?"

I know her using my first name was her way of letting me know I'd pissed her off, and now she was trying to get under my skin.

"Florida isn't a safe place for you or my daughter to be right now. But for you to understand that, I'm gonna have to take you back to where and how I met your sister."

"Well, this should be interesting. I'm all ears."

Normally, it went against my better judgement to discuss my work, but there were special circumstances. As far as I knew, I'd made a clean getaway from the mayhem I'd recently caused in Florida, but I wasn't about to tell Katie that. Instead I told her almost everything that had happened, making sure to highlight the bad people with long reaches that I'd had to eliminate. When I was done talking, she simply sat there staring out the windshield into the darkness.

"Do you understand why it's not safe for you and Kyla in Florida right now?"

"I get why you think it ain't safe, but nobody knows of our connection to you. We won't be targeted."

"You don't know that, Katie, so—"

"And you don't know that we will be, Dollar. I mean, if I have to stay out of states where you've caused havoc, then I might as well live on the fucking moon. You know it, and I know it. Nothing is gonna happen to us in Florida," she insisted.

Based on what I remembered from the time I'd spent with Katie, and what Honey had told me, I knew she had a lot of love for her dad despite his shortcomings. I was getting the feeling that this trip to Florida was about more than that though.

"I never did ask you what happened to the money you took from Eli Datton," I said.

The way her eyes quickly snapped to mine told me that I'd hit the nail on the head.

"I didn't take any money from Eli."

"You're right, you didn't, I believe it was gold bars you took and a few platinum bars as well," I replied.

The fact that I knew the specifics prevented her from kicking anymore bullshit my way, and forced her eyes back out into the darkness.

"Believe me. I earned what I took from the muthafucka. At least you had the decency to try and kill me quick, but Eli-Eli took pleasure in the fact that I was dying slowly day by day."

She spoke softly, but her words packed a power that was matched by the haunted look that had come over her face. I knew that she was no longer seeing the darkness.

"Katie, I'll take care of you and Kyla, you don't need that money the gold and platinum is worth."

"Why, because it's blood money? Well, it's my blood on it, so no one else should have it except me."

The silent tear that slid down her cheek spoke to a pain that I didn't know, but I hated it for her nonetheless. Before I could stop myself I'd pulled her out of her seat and into my lap. The way her shimmering eyes looked up at me demanded something from me, and so I gave it to her. I kissed her lips softly, seeking permission which came in the form of the salty taste of her tongue invading my mouth. There was instant heat that made the confines of the car seem smaller, but there wasn't a sense of urgency. We took our time with each other, almost like a reintroduction to something that we knew so well. I was hesitant to put my hand under her t-shirt and into the spandex shorts she had on, but when I did, the response I felt from her was immediate. It felt like I was running my fingers through hot water from a sink whose water pressure was turned all the way up. I took my time playing my melody inside her so that the rhythm would match the dance that our tongue were engaged in, and within moments the sounds of her passion were echoing off my vocal cords. I had no clear mission in mind besides allowing her to outrun her demons, but when I felt her pushing her shorts down over her hips I knew she had plans of her own.

"Hold up a second," she said.

Once she kicked her shorts off, she repositioned herself in my lap so that she was straddling me.

"Put your seat back as far as it'll go."

I followed her instructions while freeing my dick from my pants. Without hesitation, she eased herself down on top of me, and brought her mouth back to mine as she rode me nice and slow. The way she sucked my bottom lip right before she nibbled on it made my dick pound like an African drum. When I put my hands on her hip so that I could hold onto her while lifting up into her downward motion, she moved them, putting them under her shirt and on her titties instead. I wasn't surprised to find her with no bra on and the heat of her flesh rising with every passing second. When I squeezed her nipples she bit my lip, and squeezed her pussy muscles tightly around me, but her pace still didn't increase. If riding a bike was all about muscle memory, then the same had to go for riding dick, because Katie was taking me into the past right now and it was beautiful.

"G-grab my ass," she demanded softly.

I did it because I knew what it meant, and sure enough she came a few seconds later. Like the sun coming out after a storm, her climax signaled a new day, and she made me know it. She quickly pulled her t-shirt off and pulled my head to her titties, forcing me to suck her like I missed her as she went from a slow trot to a full gallop on the dick. She maintained that pace for a while, and the race was on. I bit her nipple hard just to test the water.

"Oh-fuck! I m-missed you, daddy!" she moaned, bouncing straight up and down on me.

I wanted to keep biting her, but the way she was riding me had my dick throbbing in rhythm to her pussy, and I had to concentrate on not cumming.

"K-Katie, slow down or-or I'm cumming in you."

"Oh-oh-God! I d-don't care!" she replied passionately, moving faster still.

I wanted to tell her that I cared, but it was too late because we were cumming together. Her pussy took all I had to give, and still continued to squeeze more out of me before she finally collapsed on my chest in a sweaty heap. I held her, feeling a sense of déjà vu that brought an alien feeling of guilt with it. My dick may have been inside Katie, but my mind had flashed to when Honey had been in this same position. Neither of us spoke, but I could feel how comfortable she was with me because she didn't distance herself like last time.

"I guess it's my turn to ask you why, huh?"

"Why what?" she replied, confused.

"Why did you want me to cum in you?"

"I don't know that I wanted you to, I just wasn't about to stop in order to prevent it. I mean honestly, Dollar, I don't even think I can have kids anymore, considering that no one had gotten me pregnant since you."

"What if I'm just the lucky one who can do it, and I get you pregnant again?"

My question made her lean back and look at me.

"Then I guess Kyla will have a little brother or sister won't she?"

"Oh yeah, and what about your sister?" I asked.

Something flashed in her eyes, but it happened too quick for me to interrupt, and then she smiled mischievously.

"I had you first, Dameian."

I tried to respond, but she kissed me and kept kissing me every time I opened my mouth until all I could do was laugh.

"You're still crazy, you know that?"

"Careful, Dameian, that's what you told me right before you professed your love to me the first time."

My mind immediately went back to the night she was talking about, and I could feel myself smiling. I hadn't intended to tell her I loved her, but it had felt right in the moment. Kinda like now.

"I have love for you."

The shocked expression on her face mirrored the one she'd had when I'd apologized for shooting her, and it made me laugh.

"Dameian Morgan, still full of surprises huh?"

"I'd hate to become predictable," I replied.

She kissed me again quickly before sliding off me, and back into the passenger seat. While she put her clothes back on I straightened myself, started the car, and headed back to the house. The purpose of our journey hadn't been sex, but I didn't feel like it was anything we regretted. When I pulled back up in the driveway and shut the engine off, neither of us made a move to get out, choosing to sit in the darkness a little longer.

"Dollar, what are we doing?"

"What do you mean?"

"I mean, based on what you told me, and what I've seen, you really love Tabitha. So, why do you and I keep having sex?"

She'd turned in the seat as she asked me this question, and the look on her face said she was serious about wanting an answer.

"I don't know. I feel drawn to you for some reason that I can't explain, and I know that makes no sense, because—"

"No, it makes perfect sense, because it's how I feel. I hated you, Dollar, I mean really hated you for trying to kill me, but I understood why you'd done it. Maybe that's what's allowed me to see past that hatred now, and now I just, I just want you. I haven't felt like this in years, and it scared me because I know I can't have you."

"You'll always have a part of me though," I said genuinely.

"Hopefully, that's enough."

She stared at me for a few moments before opening the door and climbing out of the car. I watched her walk inside and go upstairs before I got out and followed her into the house. I didn't go upstairs though. I went to my room and took a shower before climbing into my bed. Sleep claimed me fast and I welcomed it, hoping that my conscience let me rest without interruption. I awoke to the feeling of warm sunlight on my face and somebody shaking me gently. I opened my eyes to find Ashley sitting on the edge of the bed next to me.

"If this is your play for morning sex, you're wasting time with all those clothes on."

She didn't even crack a smile at my comment, but instead passed me a note. I read it with one eye squinting against the sunlight, but the one sentence caused both my eyes to lock on Ashley's face.

"Where's Kyla?"

"Katie took her with her and your Ferrari too," Ashley replied.

I didn't give a fuck about the car. My concern was that this bitch had taken my daughter to Florida!

"She's trying to make me kill her, huh? Wait till I catch up with her ass, I'ma—"

"You're gonna call Tabitha first, is what you're gonna do," she said.

"What? Why?"

"Because, you don't know what situation you're walking into, and you need to consult with your pregnant wife first."

Aryanna

Chapter 14
Honey
Alabama

"Hey, Mommy, what are you doing?"

"Hi sweetheart, I'm just catching up on all the news I missed during our unexpected vacation to your house. The world is so crazy. I was just reading a story about some women who died because one woman had an explosive in her you know what. That's unreal."

I was thankful that her eyes were still glued to the tablet in her hands or she might've seen the smirk on my face. One thing I loved about my husband was that he didn't lack creativity or vision when it came to his work. I took a seat beside my mom on the porch swing and laid my hand on her shoulder.

"Are you ok, sweetie?"

"I'm fine Mom, I'm just gonna miss you and the kids."

"And we'll miss you too, but it's different now than when you've left at other times. We know where you'll be, and that you'll be safe with Dollar. Plus, Christmas is right around the corner, so we'll all be together again before you know it," she said, taking my hand in hers.

"I know all of that, it's just-I like all of us being under the same roof. I'm scared, and I feel like I'm gonna need you more this time around."

She put the tablet aside before turning and lifting my chin up with her hand to make me look her in the eyes.

"Scared of what? And what do you mean you're gonna need me more this time around?"

I'd rehearsed how I would tell her that I was pregnant, but now my tongue felt like it was glued to the roof of my mouth. I had no doubt that she would embrace having another grandchild, but I had no idea how she would deal with the explanation for my fear.

"I'm-I'm pregnant, Mom."

"Okay, and are you excited about that?"

"Of course, Dollar and I planned to have another baby."

"So far, you haven't explained why you feel you need me more, or what you're scared of. I know Dollar is a flawed man, but I have the upmost confidence in his ability to take care of you and the new life that you're bringing into the world. I've seen him with Ray-Ray, Iree, Rain, and Kyla, and he's as loving as I could ever hope for when it comes to them. What aren't you telling me, sweetie?" she asked, gently.

All my life, I'd hated lying to my parents, but I'd done it to spare their feelings or to prevent them from worrying unnecessarily about me. Those lies had hurt them, and they'd hurt my relationship with them. That was something that I didn't wanna do anymore.

"Do you remember when Dollar and I didn't come straight back from our honeymoon, and he said we decided to take some extra time? Well, I'd gotten shot in a drive-by, and Dollar didn't want any of you to see me like that, so he bought a house in Florida, and took care of me."

I paused to gauge her reaction, but all I saw in her eyes was so much love through the tears that she was fighting not to let tumble. I took a deep breath before continuing.

"I-I didn't know it, but when I got shot, I was pregnant and I lost the baby. I can't put into words how much that hurt, Mom, because having a child with Dollar was something I'd secretly wanted from the first time he made love to me. I didn't know if I would get pregnant again, and now that I am, I'm afraid that I'll somehow lose this baby too."

Before she spoke she kissed me on the forehead, and laid my head back on her shoulder.

"Sweetie, I'm gonna tell you something that may be hard for you to hear, but I want you to listen with an open heart. I've never discussed what happened to me the night you were conceived because I didn't want you to hold hatred in your heart. Was it a traumatic experience? Yes, and sadly I know that that's something you understand all too well, because of your own life experiences. I was able to make peace with what happened to me because you were the blessing that came from it. God promised to turn what the devil means for bad into good, and you're living proof of that. You're living proof of God's plan, sweetheart, and no one is wise enough to question his plans. You lost a child, and while I may not know that pain intimately, I know what it's like to live in fear of losing one. It's a parent's worst nightmare, but it's not something we can let control us or we won't make the decisions that allow us to live our best lives. So, what I'm saying to you is that you have to trust in God's plan. You have to trust that for whatever reason you weren't meant to bring that first child into the world, but that this time will be different. And you have to trust that if it's not then, there's a reason for that too. There's only so much in life that you can control, and you'll drive yourself crazy worrying about the rest. I trust God with all my might, and do you know why?"

"Why?" I asked.

"Because you were the first real proof I had that miracles exist, and that made doubting him impossible for me. Just trust God, sweetie, and let everything else work itself out."

I didn't know why I was crying, but I could feel the tears sliding down my face. It always amazed me how my mother could simplify the most complicated situations by believing that everything that is meant to be will be. Even with her knowledge of the ugliness of the world and the people in it she still never asked God why he did certain things, and why he didn't do others. She just believed. I may not have had that blind faith, but I absolutely believed in my mother and the wisdom she'd accumulated over the years.

"I love you, Mommy."

"I love you more sweetie, and I trust that your husband knows how to love you in the way you need to feel safe."

"You're probably right, but first I have to tell him that I'm pregnant," I confessed.

"He already knows."

Hearing this made me raise my head quickly and look at my mother suspiciously.

"What do you mean he already knows, Mom?"

"He called a little while ago while you were in the shower and told me to tell you that Ashley told him your secret, and that he loves you. I didn't know what that meant at the time, but now it all makes sense."

"I should've known that big mouth bitch couldn't keep her lips shut," I said, shaking my head in frustration.

It hadn't been like I was planning to keep my pregnancy a secret from Dollar forever, I'd just wanted to tell him in my own way. I was definitely gonna have to smack the shit out of Ashley for fucking that up for me.

"If it's any consolation, he didn't sound mad, just a little distracted."

Hearing this had me looking at my mom differently because Dollar was too skilled at concealing his thoughts and feelings to let someone read him, especially on the phone.

"Distracted how?" I asked slowly.

"I don't know really. You can just tell when someone had a lot on their mind, and they're doing some heavy thinking."

When it came to finding out that I was pregnant that wouldn't have caused anything except happiness in Dollar, so if he was distracted then that meant something was going on. I didn't like the feeling that knowledge gave me.

"Did he say anything else?" I asked, wiping my tears off my face.

"Just that he'd see you soon."

I couldn't have agreed with him more.

"I appreciate you letting me cry on your shoulder, Mom, I needed that. I've already said bye to dad and the kids so I'm gonna get on the road so that I can celebrate with my husband."

"Sounds like a great idea. You drive safe, and make sure you call me when you get home so that I know you made it safely," she replied, pulling me towards her for a hug.

I held onto her tightly, drawing strength from the bottomless well of love that she had for me. There was no substitute for it. When I pulled back, we gently kissed each other's cheeks before I got up. I grabbed my duffle bag full of clothes out of the house, threw them in the back of the 4Runner, and then I hopped in the truck. I tried to call Dollar, but when he didn't answer, I decided to get on the move so I could surprise him. It crossed my mind to call Ashley, but I wanted to surprise that bitch too, because I had every intention of swelling up those loose ass lips of hers. After a brief stop at McDonald's, I got on the highway. Strangely, it seemed like the closer I got to home, the more excited I got about sitting down with Dollar and making the first of many plans for our baby. As usual, my mom's words had soothed me, and allowed me to see the big picture. By the time I pulled up to our house a few hours later the fear that I'd felt was forgotten, and it was replaced by enough hope to fill my heart. I got out of the truck and hurried in the house, heading straight to our bedroom because I was eager to feel my man's arms around me.

"Dollar, I—"

I pulled up short at the sight in front of me, as my brain tried to register whether or not I was seeing something real or imagined. Ashley was lying in our bed, asshole naked, with her legs spread wide and a turkey baster deep in her pussy. Next to her on the bed was a used and now empty condom.

"What the fuck are you doing?" I asked slowly.

The way she jumped told me that I'd startled her, and the look of guilt turning her face red let me know I hadn't somehow misinterpreted what I was seeing.

"H-hey Tab, what are you doing back? I thought—"

"Fuck what you thought, bitch, what the fuck are you doing?" I asked, aggressively moving towards her.

"I-I didn't have a toy handy, and I was horny, so I grabbed the first thing that I found. I'll buy you a new turkey baster, I swear."

I studied her face silently, and then looked at the entire scene again. Initially, my anger had been about this bitch doing some sneaky snake shit by trying to get herself pregnant with what I could only assume was my husband's semen, but her bullshit lies pushed me towards outright fury.

"Where's Dollar?" I asked.

"H-him and Iree went to Florida to track down Katie and Kyla. Didn't he call you?"

I immediately understood the distraction my mom had heard in my husband's voice. If Katie's dumb ass had gone to Florida with Kyla, I had no doubt she'd done it without

158

Dollar's permission, which meant she'd effectively given him another reason to kill her. The house being empty also explained why this bitch was so bold as to be in my mutha-fuckin' bed, committing the ultimate betrayal.

"So, did Dollar give you that sample of cum now swimming inside you before he left, with the instructions to get yourself pregnant? I doubt it, because if he wanted you to have his baby, he would've simply cum in you like he did me. So, what are you really doing, Ashley?"

Her eyes immediately moved to the .45 I'd pulled from the back of my shorts, and her guilt quickly transformed to fear. The turkey baster was forgotten as she swiftly sat up and put her back against the headboard.

"Tab it's-it's not what you think. I just thought it would be exciting to be pregnant at the same time as you. Think about it, our kids could grow up together, siblings and best friends all at once. It would be perfect."

"You know that all sounds plausible except for one thing, you didn't discuss any of this with me or Dollar. So, from where I'm standing, it seems more likely that being a part of my life ain't enough for you, and you actually want my life. Is that it, Ashley, you want my life and my husband?"

"N-no it's not like that, Tab, you know I love you and would never do anything to hurt you. I really just wanted to extend our family and bring us closer. Dollar has enough love to give both of us and our kids."

The fact that this crazy bitch actually believed that shit she said confirmed my suspicions. Me allowing her into our bedroom didn't mean I wanted her trying to lay claim to any part of my husband's heart. Getting the dick was one thing, but this whore wanted to elevate past the position she was brought in to play, and that was unacceptable. The sound of me pulling the slide and a bullet moving from rest to high alert echoed loudly off the walls, and caused Ashley to jump.

"Get out of my goddamn bed."

She quickly complied with my demand by getting up, but she put her back to the wall instead of moving towards me. The fact that the turkey baster was still stuck inside her would have made the situation comical if not for what it represented. To her, the turkey baster symbolized a dream or fantasy that would never be realized because to me it represented reason of the highest order.

"I loved you," I said, aiming the gun at her face.

"Tab, wait! I might-might be pregnant already! You don't wanna kill another kid."

Her words caused a cold chill to rattle my body, making the gun in my hand shake.

"I know Dollar had strong swimmers, but you just inseminated yourself, so—"

"This isn't the first time," she said softly.

It was on the tip of my tongue to accuse her of lying simply to save her ass, but I could see the truth clearly in her green eyes, and it hurt. It also solidified my decision.

"Consider this an abortion."

I lowered the gun and trained it on her pussy before I pulled the trigger. When she collapsed to the floor, I pulled the trigger two more times and sent bullets flying through her stomach. I could've let her bleed out, but I walked over to her and knelt beside her.

"I love you."

I savagely shoved the gun in her mouth and pulled the trigger a final time. After going to Dollar's office to get a new gun, I locked up the house and got back in the 4Runner. My husband didn't know it yet, but there was about to be a family reunion in Florida.

Chapter 15
Dollar
One day later

"What's the play, Pops?" Iree asked, putting the finishing touches on the blunt she was rolling.

"How many times are you gonna ask me that?"

"Until you answer me. Every time I ask you what we're doing, you give me heavy silence like I'm supposed to be able to read your mind or something. Use your words, bruh," she replied, chuckling.

If it was words she wanted, I could've easily told her I still didn't know what I was gonna do. The whole drive out here, all I kept hearing was a steady chant in my mind that said, "Kill Katie," but it wasn't that simple. I'd seen the love on Kyla's face whenever Katie came into a room. I'd heard her cry for her mommy when she was tired, because her favorite way to go to sleep was in Katie's arms. How could I take that away from my daughter? While it was true that Katie had taken Kyla away from me, she hadn't acted with malicious intent. Her one-line note saying she'd gone to Florida was nowhere near sufficient communication, and her actions were most definitely on some sneaky shit, but if she was trying to remove me from Kyla's life, she could've gone about it differently. The fact that she had my car proved that she wasn't trying to hide from me, because she was smart enough to know I could easily track it by GPS. So, how mad should I really be, because homicide mad seemed extreme right now?

"You've changed, Dollar."

This declaration caused me to turn my head in her direction and look to see if she was serious.

"Say what?"

"You heard me, I said you've changed. What happened to the Dollar who shoots first and asks questions last? Can you call him up, because this tender-dick nigga sitting beside me is not the man I know as my surrogate father."

Seeing she was being for real made me laugh heartily as I snatched the blunt from her hand and lit it.

"So, is this your way of gassing me up to kill Katie, just because you don't like her?" I asked, blowing out a cloud of smoke.

"I'm just keeping it one thousand with you. You shouldn't knock her head off simply because I don't like her, but a bitch taking your baby is a damn good reason. Shit, next thing I know you're gonna let a muthafucka kidnap me!"

I knew she'd made that statement to provoke me, but even knowing that didn't stop the anger from rising within me.

"Fuck you, Iree."

Her laughter only irritated me more, but I managed to refrain from pulling my gun and shooting her annoying ass.

"How long are we gonna sit across from this storage facility anyway?"

"Until Katie comes back out. Just relax," I replied, passing her the blunt back.

No sooner had I looked back out the windshield of the rented Lamborghini we were sitting in, then I spotted my Ferrari easing out into traffic. I quickly fired up the engine and pulled off into traffic a few car lengths behind her.

"Pull up outside the bitch and pass me your gun, I'll rock her my damn self," Iree said.

I started to pass her my pistol just to call her bluff, but the problem was that I didn't think she was bluffing.

"I got this, so just sit your little ass back and smoke, because I only brought you with me to drive one of these cars back."

"You could've brought what's her name with you for all that shit. I'm trying to get in on the action, bruh."

I decided to ignore her bullshit and keep driving. I was still trying to decide what the fuck I was gonna do, and Iree's voice was still ringing in my ears, calling me tender dick. I'd laughed it off, but I secretly feared that she was right. Just a few months ago, I was a man who cared about very little, and now it was looking like I was caring too goddamn much! I wasn't the type of nigga to find balance either. I was one way when I came to everything in life. All gas, no brakes. I put my foot down on the accelerator and quickly shifted gears, closing the distance between us and the Ferrari within seconds. When Katie suddenly turned into a restaurant parking lot, I had to swerve around her and keep going, or tap her bumper.

"Easy, before you turn two million-dollar cars into two soda cans," Iree cautioned.

I switched lanes, pulled an illegal U-turn, and doubled back. I'd expected Katie to be out of the car with Kyla, headed towards the restaurant by the time I pulled up in the parking lot, but instead she was leaning up against my car talking to a woman. At first, I thought the woman she was talking to looked familiar simply because she was attractive, but as I got closer, I realized that I knew her.

"Oh shit," I mumbled, pulling right behind my Ferrari.

"What is it?"

"Nothing, just stay in the car until I tell you to get out."

I had to resist the urge to pull my pistol out as I opened the door and climbed out, and the only reason I didn't was because I didn't wanna scare Kyla. I knew she was in the passenger seat, but I went straight to the driver's side door, catching Katie completely off guard.

"Fancy meeting you here," I said, smiling.

"Oh God," Holly murmured, as a look of terror came over her face.

I knew she was scared because the last time I'd seen her was when I'd closed the trap on her sugar daddy, who just happened to be Katie's father. I'd told her that the next time I saw her, it meant her life was about to end, but I wasn't here for her. Not this time.

"D-Dollar, what are you doing here?" Katie asked, looking around to see who was with me.

"The better question is what are you doing here, because I told you not to bring your ass to Florida."

"You-you two know each other?" Holly asked.

"He's my husband."

"Ex-husband. And right now, I'm ready to beat your hardheaded ass for bringing my daughter out here."

"Is it true that Anthony tried to kill you?" Holly asked Katie.

"Kill me? Fuck no, where did you hear that shit?"

Instinctively, I knew Holly's eyes were about to swing in my direction, so I chose to play offense instead of defense.

"We're having a private family moment, so don't you have somewhere to be?" I said, staring at Holly hard enough to melt her thinking cap.

"It's okay, Dollar, this is my dad's girlfriend, Holly. I figured she might know where my dad is, since his wife doesn't."

"Do you know where her dad is, Holly?" I asked, still staring at the visibly shaken woman.

"N-no, I was just about to-to tell Katie that he and I hadn't been really seeing a lot of each other, and then he just stopped calling me."

"Why did you ask if my dad had tried to kill me, though?"

I'd hoped that Katie was simply gonna ignore that subject, but it appeared my luck wasn't about to be that good. And if I changed the subject again, I might arouse Katie's suspicions.

"I-uh, I'd heard Anthony talking to someone who was accusing him of trying to kill his daughter. I didn't believe it, but Anthony wasn't very convincing when it came to proclaiming his innocence," Holly replied.

"My dad would never do some shit like that, not even to my sister, Tabitha, who has a volatile relationship with him."

"You-you have a sister?" Holly asked.

"Yeah, and she's my wife," I interjected.

I don't know if Katie saw the lightning of understanding flash in Holly's eyes, but I did, and I knew that my secret was safe once again.

"I never truly believed it anyway, but it's good to hear the truth from someone who loved him. I'll try to get in touch with him and let him know you're out here looking for him," Holly said.

"I don't know how long I'll be out here," Katie confessed, looking at me.

If she was expecting me to apologize for tracking her down, she had me fucked up.

"I'll text you if I hear something."

With that said, Holly quickly left us standing there as she disappeared inside the restaurant. I didn't say anything at first, because I still was uncertain of how I was gonna handle this, but the way she was smiling at me wasn't helping.

"Is this the part where you kill me, threaten to kill me, or pistol whip me right here?" she asked.

"I'm trying to remain civilized with your silly ass, but I think you're intentionally provoking me. Do I really have to tell you how bad an idea that is?"

"Dollar, relax, I didn't flee the country with our daughter, and nothing bad happened to us. Look up, the sky isn't falling."

The fact that she wasn't taking me serious, when I told her it wasn't safe for her to be out here with my daughter was pissing me off more. We both knew I was too smart to handle this situation in public though. I looked back to the Lambo and motioned for Iree to come here as I took ahold of Katie's arm.

"Oooh, you know I like it rough, don't you, daddy?" she purred seductively.

I ignored her, pushing her towards the Lambo. When she saw Iree, her smile vanished and she quickly turned to look at me.

"Follow us in my car," I told Iree.

"Wait, Kyla's in the car and—"

"And she's fine with her big sister. Now get your ass in the car before I lose my patience."

It was clear to see she had some more arguing that she wanted to do, and Iree's laughter didn't help the situation, but I knew she was smart enough to know not to push me. She took a seat in the passenger side of the Lambo, and once Iree was behind the wheel of my car, I slid in next to Katie.

"Where's your motel?" I asked.

"You knew where to find me, but you don't know that?"

"Being a smartass ain't helping the urge I have to break your pretty little face, so I'd advise you to stop testing me."

The look I levelled at her conveyed that she'd run out of rope, and she was officially about to hang herself.

"I checked out already, because I thought I'd be wherever my dad is by nightfall."

If only she knew how close she was to going in the same hole her precious father's head was in, she might think twice about her search. It was just as well though, because now I could take her somewhere private to have a much-needed conversation. I sent Aubrey a quick text telling her to let my employees know I'd be at my house in Key West in a couple hours, and then I pulled off. I drove conservatively through Fort Lauderdale until I got onto the highway, and then I turned the Lambo loose so it could eat up the road.

"Dollar, slow the fuck down, Iree is keeping pace with us and I don't want her doing a hundred and fifty miles an hour with our daughter in the car!"

I slowed down until the speedometer said I was doing a hundred miles an hour, and I set the cruise control.

"Where are we going anyway?"

"Does it matter? You got what you came out here for."

I could feel her staring at me, no doubt wondering if I was fishing or stating facts. In the end, she chose to let the subject drop, and grabbed the half of a blunt out of the ashtray, lighting it.

"I thought we had an agreement about you staying out of Florida, Katie."

"An agreement? You told me you didn't want me to go, and then we fucked, but I don't remember agreeing to anything other than you cumming in me."

"You sure you wanna be cute right now?"

"I'm being serious, Dollar, I didn't agree to shit. In fact, I told you I was coming to get what was mine, because I'd suffered for it and earned it. I thought you understood that."

"If you thought I understood, why the fuck did you sneak off after leaving me a one-line note? Why didn't you wake me up and ask me to go with you?"

When she didn't readily reply, I looked at her, but she was in deep thought while slowly smoking. I took the blunt from her fingers and filled my lungs with smoke until it was a battle to breathe and my eyes watered, before I passed it back.

"I haven't been able to depend on you or anyone else in more years than I can remember, Dollar. If it's about Kyla, I feel like I can turn to you without hesitation, and I couldn't have imagined that a month ago, but asking you for help when it comes to me…asking you to protect me, I'm not sure I know how to do that."

There was nothing I could really say to that, because I understood why she felt that way. The fact that we could be civil towards each other, co-parent, and fuck like savages didn't erase the truth when it came to me trying to take her life. The only wound that time had healed in this situation was the hole in her neck.

"To say that we've had our differences is an understatement, but for the sake of Kyla, the past has to be the past. Our daughter loves you and would be devastated if anything happened to you, so for that reason alone, I would protect you. I'm just gonna need you to stop doing shit that's gonna make me kill you."

"You ain't killing shit except this pussy and you know it, so shut up."

I tried to look at her with my most deadly expression, but it was impossible to be serious when she was smoking a blunt cross-eyed.

"You're so stupid," I said, chuckling.

"And you love me."

I left her statement hanging right in the air because the last time I confessed feeling anything like that, she felt like it gave her a license to be a renegade. I damn sure wasn't about to encourage that behavior. We managed to talk calmly for a little while, until the weed had her snoring softly. I spent the rest of the drive trying to figure out what would happen, now that some type of truce had been reached between Katie and me. My focus needed to be on Honey and the baby she was carrying, but in order for them to have my undivided attention I had to find a way to make Katie sit still. Or, at least make her stop chasing after dead men. By the time I pulled into my driveway, I had a vague idea of how to accomplish my goal.

"Katie, wake up," I said, shaking her gently.

The way her eyes fluttered open and locked on my face made my heart beat faster, and suddenly my mouth was dry.

"Come on, we're here,"

I got out of the car, and waited for her to follow my lead.

"Whose house is this?" she asked, coming to stand beside me.

"Mine."

She whistled long after hearing that.

"Okay, so maybe I didn't need the shit in the storage unit."

"I don't know, gold and platinum bars are worth an awful lot these days," I replied, looking at her.

"Will you help me turn them into cash, so I can put something away for Kyla?"

"I got you."

The smile she gave me reminded me of the girl I used to know, and before I knew it, she'd leapt into my arms.

"Girl, get your ass down before I drop you."

"You won't drop me, and I'm not getting down until we cross the threshold," she announced.

"Dad, whose house is this?" Iree asked, coming up beside us with Kyla in her arms.

"I up to Mommy," Kyla said, smiling.

"It's my house, why?"

"Yeah, I think it's about time you started giving me an allowance," Iree replied.

Katie and I both laughed at that as I walked towards the front door. I was just about to insist that Katie get down so I could open the door when it suddenly swung inward, and Honey stepped out.

Chapter 16
Honey

I could tell by the look of shock on Dollar's face that I was the last person he expected to see right now, but I'd deal with him later.

"Honey, what are you—"

"Shut up, I don't want to talk to you right now. I will have a word with you though."

I quickly grabbed a fistful of Katie's hair and pulled her out of Dollar's arms, half-dragging her into the house.

"Ow, bitch! Let go of my goddamn hair!"

Her demand only made me tighten my grip as I pulled her into the living room. When I was sure that we were out of Kyla's sight, I let her hair go so that she could stand up straight, but before she could say a word, I punched her right in her muthafuckin' mouth.

"No words, bitch, just put your hands up," I said, squaring up with her.

Without hesitation, she awakened on me, firing a jab that I blocked, followed by a hook that I ducked under. I countered with a short jab to the stomach that bent her in half, and an upper cut that took her off her feet and sent her flying through the glass coffee table.

"Nice punch," she said, quickly rising to her feet and giving me a bloody smile.

"Thank you, I've got more."

This time when she advanced, she faked throwing the hook, but my body reacted like it was real and I walked into a jab that made me taste my own blood. Her actually hitting me made me want to kill her, but I focused on hurting her first.

"You hit like a bitch," I said, dropping my guard and stepping towards her.

The fire in her eyes telegraphed her attack, making her two-punch combination look like it was coming in slow motion. I avoided her punches and timed it perfectly to hit her with a devastating left hook that brought her to her knees. Before she could get up, I had the Ruger .357 pressed to her head, with my finger on the trigger.

"Tabitha!" Dollar said sharply.

"This ain't got nothing to do with you, so stay out of it, bae."

"Don't it though?" Katie asked, chuckling.

"What the fuck is that supposed to mean, bitch?" I asked angrily.

"It means you saw me in Dollar's arms and you got jealous, but it's okay. I understand if you feel threatened."

"Threatened? By you? Why the fuck would I feel threatened by a junkie bitch that's been ran through by half the niggas in the South?" I asked, chuckling.

"Because you ain't worried about the niggas that ran through me, you're only worried that Dollar has, and he might want to again."

I told myself that her words weren't getting to me as I continued laughing, but I still found myself cocking the hammer on the gun in my hand. The only thing that stopped me from pulling the trigger was Dollar grabbing my arm and moving the gun away from her head.

"Baby, what are you doing?" he asked gently.

For a moment, I just stared at him, hating myself for searching his face for any signs of truth to what Katie had said about him possibly wanting to fuck her again, but searching nonetheless. All I saw was love and concern on his face. So, why didn't it bring the relief that it should've? I shook his hand off my arm, before tucking my gun away and walking out of the room. I made my way upstairs to the master suite and out onto the balcony, hoping that fresh air and a beautiful view would allow the savage in me to loosen its grip. My initial anger had been building since I'd left Mississippi. Here I was, supposed to be celebrating the best news of my life, but instead I'd had to hop on the highway to stop my husband from killing my impulsive ass sister. I once again had to be Captain Save-A-Hoe to her stupid ass, because she didn't know how to get out of her own way. It was a role I was used to playing, and so I'd come out here. Something about seeing the opposite of what I expected though had made me even madder. I didn't really think Dollar was, would, or wanted to stick his dick in Katie, but them being playful was somehow worse than sex to me. Them being at ease with each other likely meant they were remembering past days and happy times, and when shit like that happened, it meant Katie wasn't just my sister. She was Dollar's ex, and I saw her like I would any other bitch he used to fuck with. I'd justified my decision to put my hands on Katie mentally by telling myself she needed it for making the dumb-ass decision to come out here without permission. When I saw her in my man's arms though, she became an ex-bitch who didn't know her place, so she had to catch a fade. The question now was what did I do next? I stood staring out at the shimmering blue water searching for that answer, but I still didn't have the answer a half an hour later when I heard the door open behind me. I didn't have to turn around to know who it was, because we were connected enough for me to always feel his presence. He was my air, I was his heartbeat.

"You think our baby will have your attitude or mine?" he asked, wrapping his arms around me, and pulling me back against his chest.

"Probably both, which means the world better look out."

"Why didn't you tell me that you were pregnant, baby?"

"I was going to when I got back from Alabama. I wanted to wait until all the craziness died down so that we could focus on each other, but had I known that big mouth bitch couldn't hold water, I would've told you first."

"Are you excited?"

Hearing him ask this question made me turn around and look up at him.

"Why would you ever ask me that? You know how much it hurt me to lose our first child, and I told you to put another baby in me. We talked about it, so why would you ask me if I'm excited?"

"Because you were just downstairs throwing hands like it wouldn't have mattered if you got hit the wrong way or fell the wrong way, and a miscarriage happened," he replied logically.

"That bitch ain't never beat me in a fight, and today ain't about to be the day I let that happen. I'm beyond excited to be carrying your child, baby, so the real question is are you excited?"

His answer came in the form of him lowering his mouth to mine and kissing me tenderly. His lips and tongue conveyed so much love and I drank it all in, while giving it all back.

"Fuck me, right here," I demanded, unzipping his pants with one hand, while removing my gun with the other.

"I'm gonna have to take a raincheck on that, as tempting as it is, because we've got a situation on our hands."

"What situation?" I asked, trying to hide my disappointment.

I knew whatever it was had to be serious, because I never got denied dick.

"Katie came out here to get the gold and platinum bars she took from Eli Datton, and to link up with your sperm donor. When I caught up to her, she was talking to the last person other than me to see him alive, and I don't have to tell you how bad that could've gone."

We both knew that if Katie ever found out Dollar had killed her precious father, then any hope of civilized co-existence or co-parenting went out the window. I knew my husband, and I saw how much he loved Kyla already, so there was no doubt in my mind what he would do if Katie tried to take her from him. Death would not be merciful.

"How do you wanna handle it?" I asked.

"I'm gonna have to take care of the girl Katie met with, but that still doesn't solve the problem of her wanting to search for a dead man. So, I figured I would go to Katie with the suggestion that she call her dad's P.O. and see if he moved or something. Of course, she'll learn that her dad had violated his parole for missing appointments, and the logical conclusion she'll draw is that he's on the run."

"Which explains why she can't find him, and points out how frivolous it is to continue searching, because he could literally be anywhere," I concluded, nodding my head in agreement.

"Exactly. It should work, and within the next twenty-four hours, we should be able to put Florida in our rearview again."

Leaving Florida suddenly made me think about what exactly was waiting for us back in Mississippi.

"Well, now that you've got that figured out, I need to tell you about a little problem back home."

Despite the smirk on his face, I could tell he was curious, so I ran down what happened.

"Sneaky bitch must've kept the condom from earlier that day, but now it makes perfect sense why she insisted that I cum twice before we stopped. I thought she just wanted to fuck for a while, but she was scheming."

"Yeah, well she ain't scheming no damn more," I said, feeling anger surge through my body again at the way she'd played me.

It would never happen again though.

"If I leave first and go back to the house to clean up, then that means you'll be here with Katie. Can you deal with that?"

"I'm over that situation downstairs. At the end of the day, that's my sister and I love her, which means we're gonna go through shit and move on."

"Kinda like you and Ashley, huh?" he asked, laughing.

He'd obviously forgotten that his pants were unzipped, but when I grabbed his dick roughly the laughter got stuck in his throat. I put the pistol in my hand to the head of his dick, and looked him directly in his eyes.

"No, it's nothing like with Ashley, because if you put your dick anywhere near Katie, I'm gonna blow this mutha-fucka off and then kill you. Okay? Good talk."

I waited for him to nod his head before I released my hold on him, and let him put his dick away while I tucked my pistol into my shorts.

"You're so aggressive."

"And you love it," I replied, smiling sweetly.

"You know I do."

He took my hand in his and led me back downstairs. When we walked into the kitchen, I saw that Iree and Kyla were sitting at the table eating ice cream, while Katie held the half-gallon container of chocolate chip cookie dough to her lips. I let go of Dollar's hand, walked over to Katie, and put my arms around her.

"I love you, you hard-headed bitch."

"I love you too, but I owe you one, because my lip is swollen," she replied.

"Look at it this way, maybe it'll help you suck dick better," Iree said.

"Iree, let me talk to you real quick," Dollar said, pulling her towards the living room.

"Don't pay her any mind, she's an obvious little shit sometimes," I stated truthfully.

"That's okay, because for her fifteenth birthday, she's getting several ass whooping's, and you better not teach her how to fight before then!"

I laughed before kissing her on the cheek, and letting her go. We both loved each other too much to stay mad with one another, even after exchanging blows. At the end of the day, we were still family. I looked towards Kyla to make sure her attention was still consumed by the ice cream in the front of her before I approached the next topic with Katie.

"Dollar told me why you came out here. It's your decision to have a relationship with our sperm donor, but the way you went about coming down here was stupid and dangerous. Dollar will kill you, you know that, right?"

"Yeah, I still have the scar to prove it. I get what you're saying, and we talked about it on the drive out here. It's crazy for me to say this, but I'm actually starting to believe you were right about him changing, because he's definitely more reasonable then he was. I know he's still a killer, but I don't know, he's…different."

I should've felt relief hearing these words come from her mouth because her changing her mind about Dollar signaled less tension, and easier days for the future. I didn't feel relief though. Had the words she hurled at me earlier still not been ringing in my ears, I might not have been watching her so closely, but they were, and I was. That's how I knew that the look on her face was one of fascination, and I didn't like it because fascination led to curiosity. Sister or not, I didn't have time for no curious bitch to have her eyes on my man.

"I'm pregnant," I said, without warning.

Her eyes immediately locked on mine, and I was surprised to find disbelief in hers.

"You're pregnant? How far along?"

"Only a month. It's crazy though, because that means our baby was actually conceived in this house, so it's kinda surreal to be back here."

"Does Dollar know?" she asked, glancing in the direction he'd gone in.

"Yeah, and he's just as excited as I am. How do you think Kyla is gonna handle being a big sister?"

"Oh, I'm sure she'll love it, because I've preparing her for it since I decided that I wanted another baby."

If we'd been playing poker, I knew my expression would've given my whole hand away, but I couldn't hide the shock over hearing what she'd said.

"You want another baby? Since when, Katie?"

"Since I regained the confidence in my ability to be a good mother. Don't get on no uppity shit, like you're the only one capable of that."

Her words were delivered with a smile, but I could hear some bite in her statement.

"I've seen you with Kyla, so I know you're a good mom. I've just never heard you talk about wanting another kid, that's all. Don't get so defensive."

"I've never talked about it, because I thought I'd be in prison for a long time. Plus, it's like I told Dollar, I don't even know that I can have more kids, since I've only been pregnant once."

"You talked to Dollar about this?" I asked slowly, tilting my head and looking at her curiously.

"Not in any great detail or anything. You've gotta admit though, the way his mind works makes it easy to talk to him about anything."

"I think I liked it better when you two weren't talking," I replied.

"What the fuck is that supposed to mean, Tabitha?"

"Nothing, let's just drop it. I'm tripping, and that ain't what we need right now."

Thankfully, Dollar and Iree came back into the room so that we really didn't have to keep talking about shit that could result in another round of punches. When Iree came over to me with her arms opened wide, I turned to her and hugged her.

"Congratulations on the new baby."

"Thank you, sweetie," I replied, genuinely touched by how happy she sounded.

"You already know I'll babysit whenever you and Dollar need. That goes for you too, Katie, I'll watch Kyla whenever you want."

I heard the words, but I still had to pull back and look her in the face. Once I saw that she was all the way serious, I looked at Dollar to find him smiling at me. The shock I found on Katie's face was priceless though.

"You're joking, right?" Katie asked.

"No, that's my sister and I love her. You're her mother, and I'm gonna respect you as that."

For a moment nobody spoke, but Katie nodded her head slowly in acceptance.

"Now that that's settled, I've gotta go to work," Dollar said.

My full attention swung to him as I looked at him closely.

"Are you referring to what we discussed upstairs, or is this something different?"

"Both," he replied shortly.

"You made me a promise when it came to me being pregnant, bae—"

"And I'm gonna keep that promise. I just have a few things to handle. Iree is gonna stay here with you, and follow you home in the Lambo once you all are ready to go back to Alabama. I'm taking the Ferrari because I've got something to do for Katie."

They exchanged a look and I didn't like it, simply because I didn't understand it, but I let it slide.

"When will you be back?" I asked.

"Before you have a chance to miss me. Trust me, I got you."

Chapter 17
Dollar
Minnesota
Four days later

"Please! I'm begging you, please don't hurt my family!"

"Mr. Patell, it's not me who's hurting your family, it's you. You were the lead engineer and aeronautics architect for the Boeing 737 Max Jet, weren't you?" I asked.

"Y-yes, but—"

"And there were flaws in both the design and mechanics of the two jets that crashed, right?" I persisted.

"Y-yes, but—"

"Then, your family's suffering is your fault."

Before he could open his mouth to utter another word, I pushed his wife off the roof of their house, and watched as her body smacked the concrete patio on their backyard. It was oddly poetic how she'd landed next to the body of her twelve-year-old daughter, with her arm thrown over the girl's back like she was comforting her. Neither one of them needed comforting now though.

"Two down, two to go," I said, grabbing the five-year-old little boy by the hair, and pulling him close to me.

"I'll give you whatever! I'll give you everything I have, just please don't kill us!"

The passion in Greg Patell's pleas was gut felt and heart wrenching, but it was honestly falling on deaf ears. Standing atop this nice sized mansion more than proved that Greg had the worldly possessions to buy his freedom from anybody in the world. Well, almost anybody.

"I usually don't do this, but I'm gonna give you a choice, Greg. You can watch your son die like you did your wife and daughter, or you can jump. With your extensive knowledge of planes, you might figure out how to fly before you go splat."

"Please, I don't want—"

"You've got ten seconds to make a decision, Greg, because I'm tired, and I've got somewhere more important to be," I said, looking at my watch.

When I looked back up at him, I could see his heart in his eyes as he looked down at his son. Even in the darkness his struggle was plain to see, but I didn't really give a fuck, because I was ready to get off this cold-ass roof.

"What's it gonna be, Greg?"

"Can-can he and I jump together?"

I gave his request some thought before I turned the boy loose, and let him go to his father. The Glock .23 in my grip made sure that he didn't suddenly develop some illusion that this night ended with anything other than everybody's deaths. The trembling in his body was noticeable when he picked up his son, but he pushed through it as he broke into a sprint and flung both of them into the crisp night air. I could hear the little boy's laughter float back up to me, and I know he thought it was a game. Until it wasn't. I climbed back through the attic window and made my way downstairs to the patio. Once I saw for certain that there wasn't a heart beating between the four of them, I walked around front to the driveway, and got behind the wheel of my 2019 Black Tahoe. After I started the engine and pulled off, I grabbed my phone, and dialed the necessary number.

"It's me. It's done."

"Where to next?" Aubrey asked.

"I guess I'll get the L.A. job out of the way."

"You sound tired, Dollar."

"I am, but I'm on my way to the motel to get some sleep now. Taking all that time off has me out of conditioning when it comes to back-to-back appointments."

"I see. Why don't you take a couple days after L.A. and just rejuvenate?" she suggested.

A couple months ago, that comment would've gotten her cussed out no matter how gently she approached the subject, but I was different now. The changes in me weren't even made consciously, it just happened that being on the road didn't hold the same appeal as being home with my family. Aside from Kyla, every last one of them muthafuckas was dysfunctional, but we were still a family. And I missed them.

"Maybe you're right. I'll let you know after the business is handled."

"Safe travels," she replied, hanging up.

It took me fifteen minutes to make it to the Super 8 Motel room I'd rented, and by the time I pulled up, the not-so-comfortable bed was calling me. Before I could get out of the SUV though, my phone was vibrating in my hand, and the number calling indicated that my night could've just gotten longer.

"What's wrong, Katie?"

"Nothing, I just wanted to talk to you."

"At three a.m.? Is Kyla okay?"

"Everyone is fine, Dollar, I just have a lot on my mind and I wanted to talk to you. I thought it could wait until you get back, but according to news reports, you're moving around the country like a one-man tornado."

Her description of me made me chuckle because I did consider myself a force of nature. After silencing sweet Holly forever, I'd headed home to Mississippi to clean up my wife's mess, adding Ashley's body to the nigga who'd been stupid enough to fuck Iree in my house. Then, I got down to business, making my way across six states in the last four days, and leaving a total of twelve bodies so far. For me, it was just another day at the office, but I had no doubt that civilized society was locking their houses up a little tighter and that made me smile inside.

"Okay, well it sounds like a serious conversation, Katie, and I'm too tired for that right now, so I'll call you back in the morning."

"Tomorrow's not promised to no one, and you know that better than anyone. Beside, this conversation won't take long."

I let out a long breath in frustration as I opened the door and stepped out.

"Fine, what is it?" I asked, grabbing my gun off the seat and slipping it into my pocket.

"It's not something we can discuss over the phone."

"Well then, it really is gonna have to wait, because I'm—"

"No, it doesn't, just don't shoot me," she said.

I was about to tell her that I wasn't up for her bullshit, but the phone had hung up and I wasn't about to call her back. I closed the door of the truck, and headed for my room while digging my key card out of my pocket. I let myself in and turned on the light, and suddenly everything made sense.

"You ain't gotta worry about me shooting you, because if Honey finds out you're here, she's gonna shoot you," I said, closing the door behind me.

"Your sweet Honey is at home getting her beauty rest, and she thinks I'm visiting with some of my family on my dad's side. Our daughter is at your house, safe and sound with Iree. No one knows I'm here, and I haven't done anything to arouse anyone's suspicions."

I studied her in silence for a moment from my position by the door. The way she was reclined on her elbows on the bed with her legs crossed was effortlessly sexy, but I wasn't about to be thrown off by that. She'd obviously done some significant planning to get to where she was, and she wasn't the type to do shit without a reason behind it. Even if I didn't know that though, the look in her eyes made it clear this bitch was up to something. I grabbed the chair that sat beside the door and pushed it up against the door, before I leaned against the wall and crossed my arms over my chest.

"What do you want, Katie?"

"Nothing that should have you this paranoid."

Her laughter didn't make me crack a smile, and she quickly got the message that I wasn't in the mood to play games.

"Okay, so it's like this. I want another baby, and I want you to give it to me."

I waited for her to start laughing again, but when not even the trace of a smile crossed her face, I got a bad feeling.

"Katie, you're not serious. I know we've been getting along better, but I know you don't fuck with me on the level of having another baby with me."

"Don't I though? I know I got mad when you came inside me the first time we had sex, but that was because I was terrified to fall in love with you again. The only thing that hurt me more than you shooting me was the knowledge that I'd lost you, and ruined all the plans we'd made for the future. For a long time, it was hard to even look at Kyla, because she reminded me of you. When we fucked that first night, I was scared to relive that pain, so I didn't want to take that chance."

"So, what's changed since then? Because the last time I checked, I'm still in love with, and very much married to Tabitha."

The smile she gave me made me shiver a little, but I played it off by yawning and stretching to signal my boredom with her bullshit.

"We'll get to your marriage in a minute. What changed for me though is the fact that I've seen you've actually changed. I thought you had my sister sure enough fooled when she kept saying you were different, and you would be a good father, but I've seen the truth with my own eyes. Witnessing the man you are now opened my heart to you again, and it opened my eyes to a future I never thought possible."

"Katie, the future that you're envisioning ain't possible because I'm married to your sister."

I thought if I repeated this slowly enough and forcefully enough, it would sink into her thick ass skull, but she was smiling again as she stood up and crossed the room to me. She stared up at me for a moment, before reaching into the back pocket of her jeans, and pulling out a piece of paper that she handed to me.

"What's this?" I asked hesitantly.

"Just read it."

I unfolded the sheet of paper, and instantly recognized the marriage license issued by the state of New York for Katie Hairess and Dameian Morgan.

"Do I even want to know why you're handing me a copy of our marriage license?"

"For sentimental reasons, and to remind you of the vows we took. You did mean those vows, didn't you, Dameian? 'Til death do us part?"

"I did, until you started fucking the only man I trusted."

"I understand, and that's when you tried to separate us through death. I'm still alive though, husband."

"Congratulations, but I don't see—"

"That's because you're not thinking it through, Dameian. The day you shot me, you thought you killed me, right? Therefore it would've been pointless to file for divorce, and it probably would've only brought suspicion on you for my death, had you succeeded in killing me. We both know you're too smart for that. I also know you've never been the marrying type, so it wouldn't have crossed your mind to do any official paperwork to allow you to marry again. I'm not saying your marriage to my sister ain't legal, because Malcolm Joyner is absolutely married to Tabitha Dewhitt, but Dameian Morgan is still my husband."

I'd listened to every word she'd had to say, praying the conclusion she reached wasn't the one she was headed for. I wanted to call her a liar, but in my heart I knew she'd hit me with more truth than the stories in the Bible. As scary as the thought was, I didn't even think she'd revealed her end game yet.

"What's-what's your point?" I asked warily.

"My point is that it's only natural for a wife to want a baby by her husband. You gave Tabitha one, and now it's my turn."

I could hear the word "checkmate" echoing loudly through my head, like my brain was equipped with surround sound. I didn't feel completely boxed in yet though, so I maintained my composure while appearing to give her request the proper amount of contemplation.

"Are you saying all this to tell me that you're actually pregnant now?"

"Well, I don't know if I'm already pregnant, but I'm saying this because I have every intention on being."

"But, why would you wanna hurt your sister like that? Don't you love her?" I asked, trying to understand her thought process.

"I do love Tabitha, and if we do this right, she won't be hurt. You didn't really think I'd come this far and not have a plan, did you?"

No, I didn't think that, but that made me more afraid because it seemed like she was on some real mastermind shit.

"What's your plan, Katie?"

"Well, once I know that I'm pregnant, I'll make up an excuse to leave for a while, but I'll insist that Kyla stay with you. Tab will think I'm going back to my old life of getting high and tricking, but I'll really be going to your house in Florida. After my first trimester, I'll come back claiming not to know who my baby's daddy is, and because Tab had always taken care of me, she'll welcome me with open arms. Then we all live happily ever after."

"And what happens when our new baby comes out looking like Kyla?" I asked.

"It's natural for there to be a resemblance because they have the same mother, and if Tab says anything, I'll use the stereotype of all black people looking alike to my advantage."

She smiled as she said this, but the look in her eyes was serious.

"Seems like you've got it all figured out. There's just one thing I don't understand. What the fuck would make you think that I would go along with your crazy ass plans?" I asked seriously.

"That's easy, you still love me, and I know you love fucking me. My sister probably has some good pussy, but I'm your whore and I always will be, no matter what. Aside from phenomenal sex and blow jobs though, I'm prepared to give you something else I think you want."

If curiosity killed the cat, then I was about to lose another life.

"What do you have that I want or need so bad that I'll risk my relationship, Katie?"

"I have what you need to complete your relationship with your sweet Honey. Once I'm pregnant, you and I will very quietly get a divorce, so that you can legally marry my sister. Trust me when I tell you that she's only gonna be willing to play the role of Mrs. Malcolm Joyner for so long, especially with the constant reminder of what we had all around her. I know she loves Kyla, but do you think she looks at her and doesn't see us?"

I wasn't really into putting my hands on women, but I wanted to bop this bitch so bad right now, my mouth was watering! Standing right in front of me was the definition of what my mother had meant all those years ago about a muthafucka having too much sense, and it was hella frustrating. I think what frustrated me the most was that not one lie had tumbled from in between her lips yet, which meant that no matter how mad I got, I still had to consider what she was saying.

"I get what you're saying, Katie, but I need to think about everything you just laid on me."

"I understand, and I want you to think long and hard."

Her emphasis on those two words predicated her fingers suddenly going to the zipper of my pants, and slowly pulling it down.

"Katie, what—"

"Shhh, you're supposed to be thinking," she said, kneeling in front of me.

Within seconds, she had my dick snuggled securely in her throat and thinking was no longer possible.

Chapter 18
Honey
Mississippi
Two days later

"Good morning, my beautiful sister." I looked up from the green pepper I was chopping to see a smiling Katie breezing into the kitchen.

"You do realize it's four p.m. right?"

"I'm sorry, does me sleeping the day away bother you?" she asked, grabbing the container of orange juice from the refrigerator.

"No, it doesn't bother me. You've just been acting weird since you came back yesterday."

"Weird, how?"

The smile on her face was innocent and curious, but the twinkle in her eyes was pure mischief.

"Weird like if I didn't know any better, I'd think that you went and got some dick, instead of going to visit your family."

"Tab, you sound jealous right now."

"Jealous? Bitch, please, I got good dick on demand, so why would I be so jealous?"

For a moment she got a dreamy, far-off look in her eyes and her smile got a little bigger, but she didn't say nothing.

"Yeah, you definitely got some dick," I said, laughing.

"I did, and Tab, it was so good. It's been so long that I'd forgotten how good it was, but trust me. I'll never forget again and I made sure he wouldn't either."

"Sounds like you acted a fool on the dick, so is this the dude you plan on having a baby by?" I asked.

"I did act a fool and yes, this will be my baby daddy forever more. The way he laid pipe to me, I'm guaranteed to be under his spell until the day I die, and I ain't mad at it."

"Don't let the dick blind you to his bullshit though, because you still deserve to be treated a certain way, sis, and you shouldn't settle."

"Does Dollar's dick blind you to his bullshit?" she asked, still smiling.

"Nope, I know my baby had his flaws, and I accept them because I have mine too. I ain't gonna lie and act like what he does in that bedroom ain't a fair trade off for those flaws, but I'm still not blinded."

"He is special, isn't he?"

Her statement sounded like a compliment, but somehow it didn't make me feel that way.

"So, tell me all about this mystery man with the good dick, you can entertain me while I cook."

"I don't wanna jinx it by talking about it, but I promise you'll know everything eventually. I'll still keep you company while you're cooking though," she replied, grabbing a glass and taking a seat at the table.

I wanted to press her about her dude in hopes of discovering when or if she would be moving out, but I knew how tight-lipped she could be. It wasn't like she'd overstayed her welcome here. I just wanted her to have her own life.

"So, what are you gonna do with the money Dollar is getting you for those gold and platinum bars?"

"He told you about that?" she asked, surprised.

"Yeah, why wouldn't he? He and I don't keep secrets from each other, plus, it's not a big deal. I actually appreciate him helping you, because now you have a way to support you and Kyla when you leave."

"Leave?"

The way she spoke that one word made it sound like the idea never crossed her mind and even the suggestion of it was distasteful on her tongue.

"I mean, I just assumed with almost five million dollars in untraceable cash, you would want to spread your wings and find your place in the world."

"Oh, because my place ain't here," she said, sarcastically.

"That's not what I meant, Katie, I was simply saying that you have the means to build a wonderful life for yourself, free from the problems of yesterday. I thought you would want that for you and Kyla."

"Weren't you the someone telling me not too long ago that Dollar deserved to be in Kyla's life, and that he wouldn't let me take Kyla away from him?" she asked.

"I did, and I'm not suggesting you move away and never return. I'm simply saying that you have options now, and it would be crazy not to take advantage of them."

"I see."

I had no idea how our conversation had quickly turned into the beginning of an argument, but that was what it was starting to feel like. Instead of trying to make her understand my point, I went back to chopping up green peppers to add to the onions I would mix with the hamburger for my homemade meatloaf. Dollar was due home sometime tonight, and he would have a meal fit for a king waiting on him.

"What are you cooking, Mama Honey?" Iree asked, coming into the kitchen.

She'd taken to calling me that ever since she'd found out that I was pregnant, and it always made me smile.

"Meatloaf, mashed potatoes, corn, butter biscuits, and you already know what's for dessert."

"Ice cream and apple pie," she said, rubbing her stomach.

I laughed at the anticipation on her face.

"Where's Kyla?" Katie asked.

"Watching cartoons in her room."

True to her word, Iree had been civilized towards Katie since the cease fire was called in Florida, but whenever she spoke to her, there was still ice coating her words.

"I'll take her a snack to hold her over until dinner," Katie said, getting up from the table.

Once she grabbed some animal crackers and a Caprisun juice pouch, she left the kitchen.

"I used to think your dislike for my sister had everything to do with her presence interrupting whatever you and Rain had going on, but there's no way you'd still be mad about that. Do you wanna tell me what your real issue is with Katie?"

The moment our eyes locked, I knew I hadn't misread the situation, and Iree really did have an issue that went deeper than cock blocking on Katie's part. It didn't make sense though, because they didn't know each other, and their paths hadn't crossed when Dollar had been married to her. That meant this mystery could only be solved if Iree chose to talk about it, and I could sense her hesitation to do that.

"Is it about what she did to Dollar?" I asked.

"What she did and what she's doing."

"I don't understand. What is she doing to Dollar now?" I asked, confused.

"I feel like she's manipulating him by playing on his confused emotions. I feel like she knows how much he loves Kyla, and now that she sees that's her ticket to forgiveness she's gonna play it for everything its worth."

"What makes you think that, Iree?"

"Let's just call it women's intuition."

She stared at me hard and her eyes were saying so much, but I didn't understand. I felt like she was trying to warn me though.

"Katie ain't stupid, and she knows that trying to play Dollar will only increase the chance that he kills her. She don't wanna die."

"I love Dollar, that's my dad in every way that counts, but he's a fish out of water in this situation. He's not used to not being able to control his emotions, and if he thinks he's in control right now, he's lying to his damn self. I'm telling you, Katie is his kryptonite and he wasn't prepared for it, because he thought that she was dead."

I let her words occupy my brain as my hands moved on auto pilot, continuing to prepare dinner. I trusted her opinion and assessment, because she knew Dollar better than anyone, but in order for what she said to be true, it would have to mean that Katie was on some sneaky shit. I didn't wanna believe that, but I was all too familiar with her dope-fiend mentality. A sudden thought occurred to me that froze my hands, and made me look at my step-daughter in a new light.

"You think she wants more than a co-parenting relation-ship with Dollar, don't you?"

"I think that bitch wants whatever she can get, like any other renegade bitch that sees an opportunity."

"Nah, she wouldn't…"

Even as I was set to defend my sister, my mind went back to all the times I'd been wrong before about what she wouldn't do. I hadn't thought she'd steal from me and my kids, but she had. I hadn't thought she'd try to fuck my ex while we were still together, but her trifling ass did that too. Dollar had called me a renegade once because I'd gone rouge on him and did something without telling him. Katie was cut from a different cloth of renegade though, and I couldn't afford to be blind to her bullshit. As if on cue, she came strolling back into the kitchen carrying an empty juice container, and still walking on clouds for whatever reason.

"How's my step-daughter doing?" I asked.

"Don't call her that," Katie snapped immediately.

"Why not, it's true? Beside, Mama Honey is a wonderful stepmother and I wouldn't ask for one better," Iree said, smiling at me.

"If you want her to be your stepmother, that's fine, but she's Kyla's aunt and that's how I'm gonna raise my daughter to see her."

"Won't it get confusing once I have my baby though?" I asked innocently.

"Are you gonna say that's her cousin, or her brother or sister?" Iree asked.

"How about we wait until you actually have Dollar's baby, and then we can have this discussion, because right now it's pointless."

"Pointless? No, I think it's good to get an understanding before our baby gets here. I mean, I'd be willing to talk to you about your baby if you were pregnant right now," I said.

"I might be pregnant," Katie blurted out, smiling.

I started to laugh at her, but the way Iree spun around and advanced on her stopped me. Before I could utter a word, Iree had a handful of Katie's hair and she was using her other hand to speak sign language to her face. The sound of the first punch landing made me cringe, and I knew that Katie's warning to me about teaching Iree how to fight was wasted breath, because my step-daughter had hands. A second punch quickly followed the first and I saw Katie's knees try to buckle, but Iree held her up by her hair long enough to throw a knee into her stomach.

"Iree," I said.

She turned and looked at me, and I shook my head to stop her from continuing. I could see the reluctance on her face, but she let Katie go and took a step away from her. I quickly moved around the kitchen counter because I knew my sister, and I got to her just in time to stop her from lunging at Iree.

"Get the fuck out the way, Tab, I'ma beat that little bitch!"

"That ain't happening and you know it. She's just a kid, Katie."

"I hit like I'm grown though," Iree said, laughing.

Her comment made Katie try to lunge through me to get at her, but I managed to keep them separated.

"Get the fuck off me!" Katie screamed, pushing me backwards into Iree.

"You're gonna put your hands on her, knowing she's pregnant? Outside, bitch, now!"

Iree's tone made me look at her, and it was like seeing a female version of Dollar. It was obvious she was hell-bent on teaching Katie a lesson, and I was gonna let her.

"I'll gladly take it outside," Katie said, putting her hair in a ponytail while heading for the door.

"Iree, you—"

"Nah, I got this, and it needs to happen."

She quickly put her hair in a ponytail too and pulled off her t-shirt, revealing her sports bra, before following Katie outside. I checked to make sure my pistol was still secured in the back of my shorts, and then I went outside too. By the time I made it to the front porch, they were already squared up in the grass. Neither of them spoke a word. They got straight to the action. Iree's size and reach advantage was clear, because she looked like a five-foot-seven-inch giant next to Katie's five-foot-three-inches, but Katie used her speed to slip within firing range and landed two mean body blows. Her mistake was over-confidence though, because instead of backing up, she assumed her punches would leave Iree bent over, so she was already throwing her uppercut. With Iree still standing up straight, she saw the punch coming from a country mile, allowing her to side step and fire her own two punches that put Katie on her ass.

"Get up, bitch, we're just getting started."

Pride made Katie comply immediately, but instead of throwing another punch, she rushed Iree and turned the fight into a ground game. The advantage changed swiftly with Katie throwing a flurry of punches to Iree's face that resulted in blood flying. I wanted to intervene, but I knew I had to be fair and let the situation play out. When Iree locked her legs around Katie's waist and rolled her, I knew I'd been worried for no reason. The punches she landed once she had Katie on her back caused me to feel real fear for my sister though. I treated it like a UFC fight, which meant that as long as Katie was putting up an adequate defense, I would let them go. That only lasted a few more moments though, because Iree landed a right hook flush to Katie's chin, and I could suddenly hear her snoring from where I stood.

"That's enough," I said.

Iree didn't throw another punch, but she did spit blood in her face before climbing off of her and walking towards me.

"I underestimated you because you're young, but it's clear you've had to knock some sense into a bitch before."

"The bully always wants to test the pretty girl who's popular, and I had to show them why that was a bad idea."

When she stopped in front of me, I took her face in my hands and gave it a close inspection. Her lip was busted, her nose was bleeding, and she had a small cut under her left eye, but she was all smiles.

"You did good, daughter," I said with pride.

"Thanks, Mama Honey. We don't tolerate no renegade bitches who fuck other people's men."

For a second, I just stared at her as I processed what she'd said. When she tried to move past me to go in the house, I stopped her.

"Iree, whose man did she fuck? What aren't you telling me?"

Aryanna

Chapter 19
Dollar

The word tired didn't even begin to explain how my body felt. Despite my lean, somewhat muscular figure, I felt completely out of shape for all the activities I'd engaged in over the past seventy-two hours. Adding another seven people to my body count had taken a lot out of me, but adding Katie's insatiable freakiness to the mix made me want to hibernate for the next nine months. Since her sudden return from the dead, our two sexual encounters had been rather mild, but when she showed up at my motel she brought all the tricks from our past with her. We fucked and sucked each other like we were trying to pull the soul out of one another. I'd literally lost an entire day, because she wouldn't quit. It didn't matter that her pussy had swelled up to the point that it hurt, or that there had been some tearing with regards to her asshole, she still wouldn't let me stop. And when she physically couldn't take the dick anymore, she popped it in her mouth and drank enough cum to fill up her stomach twice! She'd been determined to prove that she was my whore, and prove it she did. I was suffering for it now though, because I felt like a zombie in need of a lot of rest. It was for this reason I'd cut my business trip short and returned home earlier than what I'd told Honey to expect. Despite my time with my other wife, I was hoping to surprise her. When I pulled up in front of the house, and saw Honey and Iree standing on the porch steps while Katie laid in the grass, I knew it was me who was in for the surprise though. I could see the blood on Iree's face, which explained the scene without words being necessary. I was already shaking my head as I climbed out of my car, but Iree was all smiles. The look on Honey's face was unreadable, and that made me feel uneasy.

"You just couldn't help yourself, could you?" I asked, stopping at the bottom of the steps.

"She deserved it and you'd know that, if you weren't so blind," Iree said.

"What the fuck is that supposed to mean?" I asked aggressively.

"Nothing, just forget it."

Before I could say anything else, she'd turned around and gone in the house.

"You wanna tell me what that was about, bae?"

"Honestly, I'm still trying to figure it out myself. What I do know is that Iree doesn't trust Katie, and she believes Katie had a hidden agenda. Why do you think that is, husband?"

The change in her tone was subtle, but it was still easy to tell when it changed from conversational to accusatory, and my guard immediately went up.

"It sounds like you're asking me something deeper than that superficial shit you just came with, wife, so what's really going on?"

"That's what I want to know, what's really going on?"

"Put your big girl panties on, Tabitha, and be specific."

"Ok, are you fucking my sister?"

"You know the answer to that question."

"What I know is that you didn't answer the question, Dameian, so let's try this again. Are you fucking my sister?"

"No."

I'd hoped my lack of hesitation, coupled with the fact that I hadn't gotten defensive, would convince her that I was telling the truth, but I could see the wheels of suspicion spinning behind her eyes. I may not have known the full extent of the shit I'd stepped into when I pulled up, but it was clear to me now that I'd absolutely stepped into some shit.

"Did Kyla see any of this?" I asked, trying to shift the focus.

"No, your daughter is upstairs watching TV, maintaining her innocence."

"My daughter," I repeated slowly.

"Yeah, Katie said she doesn't want me to refer to her as my step-daughter because I'm her aunt, and that's how she'd gonna raise her."

"From the attitude I hear in your voice, I can tell that you really took that to heart, which is crazy. You're my wife and by definition, that makes you Kyla's stepmom."

"Does it though? I mean, I'm Malcolm Joyner's wife, and Malcolm doesn't have any kids, except for the one I'm carrying right now. Kyla belongs to Dameian Morgan."

In my ears, I could suddenly hear Katie's words, spoken to me in my motel room, and I wondered if she'd said anything to Honey. It was obvious that at the very least, Katie had been antagonizing one, if not both women and that's why she was currently catching a nap in the grass. If she'd told it all though, she would've been resting permanently, so I knew Honey could only know so much.

"Since when did you start separating me by name?" I asked.

"Not until your ex-wife felt the need to point it out by making the statement that she did. Shit got more interesting though when Iree asked her if our baby would be raised as Kyla's cousin or sibling, because that's when she insisted that I actually have a baby by you before we had that conversation. When I expressed to her my belief that we should have certain shit established before our baby was born, and that I would've offered her the same courtesy if she was pregnant, she informed me that she might be pregnant."

I kept my facial expression completely neutral, because I knew her pause in speech was intentionally to gauge my reaction. Inside, I wanted to go punch Katie in the face my damn self, because the way she was moving was not what we'd agreed upon. She was damn near taunting Honey! It was a wonder Honey hadn't shot her.

"Okay, and?" I asked, once the silence began to drag on.

"And the last comment is what caused Iree to whoop her ass. Don't you think it's odd that Katie announcing the possibility of being pregnant would set Iree off like that?"

"Only if you're looking for it to be odd. The simple and logical explanation is that Iree had every intention on fighting her at some point, but she didn't wanna wait nine months to do it. In case you've forgotten, my daughter is impulsive."

"Maybe you're right. I'm surprised that you're home early, it's almost like Katie sent you an SOS to save her."

"You're funny, bae. I'm home early because I missed you, but based on the amount of space still between us, I'm thinking you don't feel the same way."

She stood there staring at me for a couple more seconds before walking down the steps towards me. She stopped on the last step, which put us almost at eye level.

"How much space do you want between us?"

I answered her question by pulling her towards me roughly and kissing her hard. Our tongues didn't battle for domination as usual. Mine simply took control and refused to relinquish it no matter what she did. It was my intention to fuck her right here on the front steps, but her tapping me on the chest made me pull back and look at her.

"If my pussy gets any wetter, that's all you'll have to eat tonight, because I haven't finished dinner yet. And before you say it, no, I'm not gonna let everyone else starve just so you can eat."

I smiled because she knew me so well, but I nodded my head in understanding before I kissed her again quickly.

"How long will it take you to finish dinner?"

"A couple hours, but while I'm doing that, you can clean your baby mama up before Kyla sees her."

"I'll take care of it," I replied, releasing her from my embrace.

I watched her walk up the stairs so I could admire her ass, and then I turned to go get Sleeping Beauty from amongst the dandelions.

"She definitely beat your ass, huh?" I questioned aloud, shaking my head. I scooped her up into my arms and carried her into the house. I didn't want to take the risk of Kyla seeing us if I went upstairs, so I carried her into one of the spare bedrooms on the first floor, and laid her across the bed. After grabbing a washcloth and running warm water over it, I returned to her side, and gently begun to clean her face. The feeling of the wet rag on her skin made her eyes flutter open, but when she saw it was me attending to her, she closed them again.

"You're being reckless, Katie."

"I know."

"But why, I thought we talked about this. To intentionally goad Honey or Iree is dumb, and you're not dumb, so what are you doing?"

Her eyes opened again and locked on mine.

"I love you, Dameian, and I don't know if I can share you. I thought I could, but I really don't know."

I didn't know what to say, so I just kept cleaning her cuts until her face was no longer a red mess.

"I think your nose might be broken."

"It is, but it's not the first time. I want you to reset it."

"Katie, that's gonna hurt."

"It'll hurt more later, so just do it."

She moved her head into my lap and closed her eyes. I grabbed ahold of her nose and twisted until it was back in a straight line. The sound of her high-pitched scream, accompanied by the sound of her nasal bones grinding, let me know that she was officially realigned.

"No more fighting, Katie, I'm serious."

She brought her index finger to her lips and tapped them twice to indicate that she wanted a kiss. I could hear Honey moving round in the kitchen, but I still looked up to make sure no one was standing in the doorway. With the coast clear I brought my lips down to hers gently intending to give her a peck, but she opened her mouth to me and demanded I do the same. For a moment I was lost, but I pulled back before it could go too far.

"We can't take chances like this with your sister around," I whispered.

Her stare was intense, but she nodded her head in understanding before sitting up and taking the washcloth from my hand. Without a word, she left the room while I sat there, trying to figure out how to avoid this type of mess in the future. One thing I knew for sure was that this house was not big enough for all of these women to co-exist. I knew how to fix that though, and I took my idea with me into my own bedroom, so I could further contemplate it while I took a shower. The hot water was relaxing and it served to take away some of the fatigue I felt. I spent a long half-hour under the water's therapy before getting out, feeling reinvigorated. I dressed quickly and went to my office to get some work done, because I figured I was in for a long night of activities to take Honey's mind off of her sister's bullshit.

"Are you mad at me or can I come in?" Iree asked from the doorway.

"You can come in, but don't mean I ain't mad at you."

Even though she had her hands behind her back, I could still see the smoke floating up behind her, and I could smell the weed. I wasn't surprised when she passed me the blunt before taking a seat across from me.

"Do you wanna hear my side of the story?" she asked.

"I know your side. Katie said what she said, and you knew what it meant. I wish you would've controlled your reaction to it, though."

"You can't get her pregnant, Dollar. First of all, you know what that would do to Honey and I don't think you wanna hurt her that way. Plus, you know that Katie ain't shit, so why tie yourself to her even more than you already have?"

It was on the tip of my tongue to explain that she had no idea how tied to Katie I actually was, but I didn't see how revealing that secret would help.

"This whole situation is complicated but trust me, I hear what you're saying, daughter."

"Then fix it before it's too late."

With that said, she stood up and left me alone with my thoughts floating around like the weed smoke. I gave my situation serious analyzation as I puffed and before I knew it, the blunt was long gone, but I was still stuck in my chair wrapped up in deep thought. A future that was all sunshine and rainbows a short while ago was now tinged with clouds that threatened to bring one hell of a storm. The climate change was real.

"Dinner's ready," Honey said from the doorway, startling me out of my thoughts.

"Okay, baby, I'll be right there." Once she left, I took a few seconds to put my game face back on before I followed her to the dining room. I was surprised to find everyone in attendance, but my focus immediately went to Kyla, who was opening her arms to me for a hug. I immediately scooped her up and covered her face with kisses, which made her giggle.

"You miss your daddy?" I asked.

Before she could answer, my phone started ringing in my pocket. I put Kyla back in her chair while pulling it out, and I answered without looking, because I knew who it had to be.

"I'm about to eat, Aubrey, and you know—"

"Your wife is under code black. Run."

My eyes immediately swung towards Honey. Aubrey constantly monitored law enforcement databases worldwide for any mention of any of my aliases, and when Honey had gotten shot, I'd had Aubrey add her name to that list. Code black meant that her name hadn't simply popped up. It meant the law was coming for her.

Chapter 20
Honey

The way Dollar looked at me froze my chaotic emotions in my chest, because I knew whatever that phone call was didn't have shit to do with him and my sister.

"What?" I asked.

"Come with me."

He didn't even want to see if I would follow, before he let go of Kyla, and headed in the direction of his office.

"Iree, bring all the food to the table, and no fighting while I'm gone," I instructed, following Dollar.

"I got you, Mama Honey."

By the time I made it to the office, Dollar was already sitting at his desk in front of the laptop with his fingers flying over the keyboard, and a look of pure concentration on his face.

"Bae, what's wrong?"

"Aubrey called and said the cops are coming for you."

"Cops? For what?" I asked in disbelief.

"That's what I'm trying to find out now, hold on."

While he continued to put his cyber wizard skills to use, I wondered what the hell the cops could be after me for. It wasn't like I believed there was a case of mistaken identity. I was more so wondering which crime they thought they had me for. Even as I asked myself the question, my mind went back to the night in Kentucky that I still wished I could forget. I knew I didn't deserve to forget though. I deserved to be haunted by it for the rest of my life.

"Oh fuck," Dollar mumbled, slumping back in his chair.

"What is it?"

He pointed to the laptop's screen, and I moved to his side so that I could see it. He had dashcam footage pulled up from a police traffic stop, and as soon as I saw the cops head explode, I knew what I was looking at. I'd grabbed the cop's body cam, but I forgot about the dashcam. I watched with growing horror as I got out of the car and secured his body, and then shot the nurse who'd been trying to escape. I knew it was me because I'd been there, and Dollar knew it was me because I told him, but at no point did I ever fully face the cop's car and dashcam.

"Dollar, they shouldn't have identified me from this footage."

"Huh?"

"I said they should not have been able to identify me from this footage, look at it closely."

He rewound it and watched it once, and then again. After watching it completely a third time, he put his fingers back to work with lightning speed. I had no idea what he was looking for, but something about this situation stank.

"They've issued a warrant for your arrest in the name of Tabitha Joyner."

"But, how is that possible, bae? If Tennessee ran my picture against that video and identified me, they'd still come up with my maiden name in their system. They shouldn't know my name or where I am because I'm not on probation, so I don't have to check in with anyone."

"Which means there's only two ways for them to know, and since the charges are two counts of capital murder, that means the nurse didn't survive to give a statement."

"But, somebody did," I said, looking at him.

The truth was written all over his face, but the sound of approaching sirens made it irrelevant for the moment. He quickly hopped up out of his chair and went to his bookshelf, opening a false panel. I heard him pressing numbers on a key pad, and then he shut the panel before going to the safe.

"What's the play, baby?"

"Make it out of here alive and not in police custody. Take these," he replied, passing me a set of car keys I'd never seen before.

"Where's this car, out back?"

"Come with me and I'll explain," he said, pulling two Glock 9mm's from the safe and closing it.

He quickly led the way back into the dining room, where he passed a gun to Iree.

"You know where the door for the tunnel is, right?" he asked.

"Is this a test, Dad, because you know—"

"Those sirens you hear are headed straight for us, so this is not a test," he replied seriously.

"The door is under the huge wine rack at the far end of the basement. I press a button along the left side panel and the wine rack moves out of the way, and then I punch in the password on the keypad that's on the door to the tunnel," Iree recited, tucking the pistol into the back of her shorts.

"Take Kyla with you. You're driving the Audi R6, and I want you to go straight to the house in Florida. There's money in the glove box and a cellphone that has Aubrey's number programmed. Call her when you're safely away from here," Dollar instructed, passing her the other set of car keys.

"I love you, Dad."

"I love you too, daughter."

They exchanged a quick hug, and he made sure to hug and kiss Kyla too, before Iree picked her up and disappeared out of the dining room.

"Dollar, what the hell is going on, why are we running?" Katie asked.

"Because the cops are coming and if they're coming for one of us, then they're coming for all of us."

"Ok, well, where's my gun in case we have to bang it out with them? Because, I am not going back to prison."

"Just stick with me, I got you," I told her.

I could tell by the way she looked at Dollar that she would've preferred that statement come from him, but before she could say anything, the lights went out. Within a few seconds, a backup generator began humming and partial light was restored.

"Was that supposed to happen?"

"Yeah, it means the property has officially been breached, and it's now armed," he replied.

"Armed?" Katie asked.

"Yeah, there are land mines buried all over, which is one of the reasons we're not about to try and escape out the front or the back."

"How solidly built is this tunnel of yours?" I asked warily.

"Don't worry, my cartel connect did it for me, and no expense was spared. It runs all the way to the property to the west, which I own under a different name."

"For the first time, I'm glad your ass is OCD," Katie said, chuckling.

"So, what are we waiting on?" I asked.

"I'm giving the kids a head start, plus I wanna see the fireworks," he replied, smiling.

Before I could ask what he meant, a sound reminiscent of cannon fire reached my ears, and caused the ground to tremble slightly. Outside, it suddenly looked like time had sped up because an orange glow lit the sky like the sun was rising. Seconds after the first explosions, two more went off simultaneously and this time, the ground moved like we were standing on top of shifting plates, close to the Earth's core.

"You've had your fun, now let's get the hell out of here," I said, pulling my gun out.

Dollar laughed, but he led the way down to the basement where we found the door to the tunnel open and waiting. He sent me down the ladder first, and I was surprised to find enough room to move around comfortable upright, plus there were lights everywhere. I waited for Katie and Dollar to get to ground level, and then Dollar led the way. We moved swiftly, and I could barely make out the sounds of continuing explosions after a few minutes. Ten minutes later, we came to another ladder that led up into an empty basement, and I breathed a sigh of relief to be above ground again.

"Honey, you've got the keys to the Camaro, so you drive," Dollar said, closing the tunnel door, and turning towards me.

I didn't move, I simply stared at him. I'd never known a love like the one he constantly demonstrated, and I was positive I never would again.

"Baby, why are you crying?" he asked.

I hadn't realized I was, but now that he'd mentioned it, I could feel the tears sliding slowly down my face.

"Why did you fuck her, Dollar? After everything she did, why fuck her?" I asked.

"Baby, I didn't—"

"Yes, you did, and the proof is in the fact that she told the cops where to find me. She wants me out of the picture so she can have you, but she doesn't deserve you, I deserve you."

"Why don't I deserve him, bitch? I had him first."

My answer to her question came with me turning towards her and shooting her twice in the chest, before calmly turning my attention back to my husband.

"Why, Dollar?"

"I don't know, baby, I really don't. I love you with all of my heart, and I could never love anyone the same way I swear."

"She never deserved you, but I did though. I did," I said, crying harder.

He took a step towards me, and I shot him in the chest. I could see the shock on his face as I stood over him, but I didn't know why he was surprised, because I'd warned him.

"I love you, Dameian."

"I-I love you, Hon—"

My next shot silenced his lie.

"I deserved you…"

To Be Continued…
Soul of a Monster 3
Coming Soon

Submission Guideline

Submit the first three chapters of your completed manuscript to ldpsubmissions@gmail.com, subject line: Your book's title. The manuscript must be in a .doc file and sent as an attachment. Document should be in Times New Roman, double spaced and in size 12 font. Also, provide your synopsis and full contact information. If sending multiple submissions, they must each be in a separate email.

Have a story but no way to send it electronically? You can still submit to LDP/Ca$h Presents. Send in the first three chapters, written or typed, of your completed manuscript to:

LDP: Submissions Dept
Po Box 870494
Mesquite, Tx 75187

DO NOT send original manuscript. Must be a duplicate.

Provide your synopsis and a cover letter containing your full contact information.

Thanks for considering LDP and Ca$h Presents.

Coming Soon from Lock Down Publications/Ca$h Presents

BOW DOWN TO MY GANGSTA

By **Ca$h**

TORN BETWEEN TWO

By **Coffee**

BLOOD STAINS OF A SHOTTA **III**

By **Jamaica**

STEADY MOBBIN **III**

By **Marcellus Allen**

RENEGADE BOYS IV

By Meesha

BLOOD OF A BOSS **VI**

SHADOWS OF THE GAME II

By **Askari**

LOYAL TO THE GAME **IV**

LIFE OF SIN **III**

By **T.J. & Jelissa**

A DOPEBOY'S PRAYER **II**

By **Eddie "Wolf" Lee**

IF LOVING YOU IS WRONG... **III**

By **Jelissa**

TRUE SAVAGE **VII**

By **Chris Green**

BLAST FOR ME **III**

DUFFLE BAG CARTEL **IV**

HEARTLESS GOON **II**

By **Ghost**

A HUSTLER'S DECEIT III

KILL ZONE **II**

BAE BELONGS TO ME III

SOUL OF A MONSTER III

By **Aryanna**

THE COST OF LOYALTY **III**

By **Kweli**

A GANGSTER'S SYN III

By **J-Blunt**

KING OF NEW YORK V

RISE TO POWER III

COKE KINGS III

By **T.J. Edwards**

GORILLAZ IN THE BAY IV

De'Kari

THE STREETS ARE CALLING II

Duquie Wilson

KINGPIN KILLAZ IV

STREET KINGS III

PAID IN BLOOD II

Hood Rich

SINS OF A HUSTLA II

ASAD

TRIGGADALE III

Elijah R. Freeman

MARRIED TO A BOSS III

By Destiny Skai & Chris Green

KINGZ OF THE GAME IV

Playa Ray

SLAUGHTER GANG III

RUTHLESS HEART

By Willie Slaughter

THE HEART OF A SAVAGE II

By Jibril Williams

FUK SHYT II

By Blakk Diamond

THE DOPEMAN'S BODYGAURD II

By Tranay Adams

TRAP GOD

By Troublesome

YAYO

By S. Allen

GHOST MOB

Stilloan Robinson

KINGPIN DREAMS

By Paper Boi Rari

CREAM

By Yolanda Moore

Available Now

RESTRAINING ORDER **I & II**

By **CA$H & Coffee**

LOVE KNOWS NO BOUNDARIES **I II & III**

By **Coffee**

RAISED AS A GOON I, II, III & IV

BRED BY THE SLUMS I, II, III

BLAST FOR ME I & II

ROTTEN TO THE CORE I II III

A BRONX TALE I, II, III

DUFFEL BAG CARTEL I II III

HEARTLESS GOON

A SAVAGE DOPEBOY

HEARTLESS GOON

By **Ghost**

LAY IT DOWN **I & II**

LAST OF A DYING BREED

BLOOD STAINS OF A SHOTTA I & II

By **Jamaica**

LOYAL TO THE GAME

LOYAL TO THE GAME II

LOYAL TO THE GAME III

LIFE OF SIN I, II

By **TJ & Jelissa**

BLOODY COMMAS I & II

SKI MASK CARTEL I II & III

KING OF NEW YORK I II,III IV

RISE TO POWER I II

Aryanna

COKE KINGS I II
BORN HEARTLESS
By **T.J. Edwards**
IF LOVING HIM IS WRONG…I & II
LOVE ME EVEN WHEN IT HURTS I II III
By **Jelissa**
WHEN THE STREETS CLAP BACK I & II III
By **Jibril Williams**
A DISTINGUISHED THUG STOLE MY HEART I II & III
LOVE SHOULDN'T HURT I II III IV
RENEGADE BOYS I II III
By **Meesha**
A GANGSTER'S CODE I &, II III
A GANGSTER'S SYN II
By **J-Blunt**
PUSH IT TO THE LIMIT
By **Bre' Hayes**
BLOOD OF A BOSS **I, II, III, IV, V**
SHADOWS OF THE GAME
By **Askari**
THE STREETS BLEED MURDER **I, II & III**
THE HEART OF A GANGSTA I II& III
By **Jerry Jackson**
CUM FOR ME
CUM FOR ME 2
CUM FOR ME 3
CUM FOR ME 4

220

CUM FOR ME 5

An **LDP Erotica Collaboration**

BRIDE OF A HUSTLA **I II & II**

THE FETTI GIRLS **I, II& III**

CORRUPTED BY A GANGSTA I, II III, IV

BLINDED BY HIS LOVE

By **Destiny Skai**

WHEN A GOOD GIRL GOES BAD

By **Adrienne**

THE COST OF LOYALTY I II

By Kweli

A GANGSTER'S REVENGE **I II III & IV**

THE BOSS MAN'S DAUGHTERS

THE BOSS MAN'S DAUGHTERS II

THE BOSSMAN'S DAUGHTERS III

THE BOSSMAN'S DAUGHTERS IV

THE BOSS MAN'S DAUGHTERS **V**

A SAVAGE LOVE **I & II**

BAE BELONGS TO ME **I II**

A HUSTLER'S DECEIT I, II, III

WHAT BAD BITCHES DO I, II, III

SOUL OF A MONSTER I II

KILL ZONE

By **Aryanna**

A KINGPIN'S AMBITON

A KINGPIN'S AMBITION **II**

I MURDER FOR THE DOUGH

By **Ambitious**

TRUE SAVAGE

TRUE SAVAGE II

TRUE SAVAGE **III**

TRUE SAVAGE **IV**

TRUE SAVAGE **V**

TRUE SAVAGE **VI**

By **Chris Green**

A DOPEBOY'S PRAYER

By **Eddie "Wolf" Lee**

THE KING CARTEL **I, II & III**

By **Frank Gresham**

THESE NIGGAS AIN'T LOYAL **I, II & III**

By **Nikki Tee**

GANGSTA SHYT **I II &III**

By **CATO**

THE ULTIMATE BETRAYAL

By **Phoenix**

BOSS'N UP **I , II & III**

By **Royal Nicole**

I LOVE YOU TO DEATH

By Destiny J

I RIDE FOR MY HITTA

I STILL RIDE FOR MY HITTA

By **Misty Holt**

LOVE & CHASIN' PAPER

By **Qay Crockett**

TO DIE IN VAIN

SINS OF A HUSTLA

By **ASAD**

BROOKLYN HUSTLAZ

By **Boogsy Morina**

BROOKLYN ON LOCK I & II

By **Sonovia**

GANGSTA CITY

By **Teddy Duke**

A DRUG KING AND HIS DIAMOND I & II III

A DOPEMAN'S RICHES

HER MAN, MINE'S TOO I, II

CASH MONEY HO'S

By Nicole Goosby

TRAPHOUSE KING **I II & III**

KINGPIN KILLAZ I II III

STREET KINGS I II

PAID IN BLOOD

By **Hood Rich**

LIPSTICK KILLAH **I, II, III**

CRIME OF PASSION I & II

By **Mimi**

STEADY MOBBN' **I, II, III**

By **Marcellus Allen**

WHO SHOT YA **I, II, III**

Renta

GORILLAZ IN THE BAY **I II III**

DE'KARI

TRIGGADALE I II

Elijah R. Freeman

GOD BLESS THE TRAPPERS I, II, III

THESE SCANDALOUS STREETS I, II, III

FEAR MY GANGSTA I, II, III

THESE STREETS DON'T LOVE NOBODY I, II

BURY ME A G I, II, III, IV, V

A GANGSTA'S EMPIRE I, II, III, IV

THE DOPEMAN'S BODYGAURD

Tranay Adams

THE STREETS ARE CALLING

Duquie Wilson

MARRIED TO A BOSS… I II

By Destiny Skai & Chris Green

KINGZ OF THE GAME I II III

Playa Ray

SLAUGHTER GANG I II

By Willie Slaughter

THE HEART OF A SAVAGE

By Jibril Williams

FUK SHYT

By Blakk Diamond

DON'T F#CK WITH MY HEART I II

By Linnea

ADDICTED TO THE DRAMA I II III

By Jamila

<u>BOOKS BY LDP'S CEO, CA$H</u>

<u>TRUST IN NO MAN</u>

<u>TRUST IN NO MAN 2</u>

<u>TRUST IN NO MAN 3</u>

<u>BONDED BY BLOOD</u>

<u>SHORTY GOT A THUG</u>

<u>THUGS CRY</u>

<u>THUGS CRY 2</u>

<u>THUGS CRY 3</u>

<u>TRUST NO BITCH</u>

<u>TRUST NO BITCH 2</u>

<u>TRUST NO BITCH 3</u>

<u>TIL MY CASKET DROPS</u>

<u>RESTRAINING ORDER</u>

<u>RESTRAINING ORDER 2</u>

<u>IN LOVE WITH A CONVICT</u>

<u>Coming Soon</u>

BONDED BY BLOOD 2

BOW DOWN TO MY GANGSTA

Aryanna

www.ingramcontent.com/pod-product-compliance
Lightning Source LLC
Chambersburg PA
CBHW070451260626
47161CB00004B/1269